GABRIELLE KENT

The SECRETS of HEXbRIDGE CasTLE

SCHOLASTIC INC.

First published in the United Kingdom in 2015 by
Scholastic Children's Books, an imprint of Scholastic Ltd., London

ISBN 978-1-338-16619-4

12 11 10 9 8 7 6 5 4 3 2 1   17 18 19 20 21 22

Printed in the U.S.A.   40

This edition first printing, January 2017

Book design by Carol Ly

For Satish,
for yesterday and tomorrow.

Mrs. Emmett's Visitor

There were many things Nora Emmett disapproved of. These included whistling, tropical fruit, sandals, children who didn't hold doors open for her, children who assumed she *needed* doors opening for her—in fact she pretty much disapproved of children altogether. However, at this moment as she sat up in bed listening to the darkness, the thing she disapproved of most of all was whatever had woken her at three o'clock in the morning.

She didn't have long to wait before the sheep started bleating again. Reaching out into the darkness, she struck a match and lit the oil lamp on the nightstand with an uncanny accuracy that came from years of practice. Mrs. Emmett didn't quite trust electricity yet.

The brass bedstead creaked as she got up, wriggled into her tartan slippers, and shuffled downstairs to investigate.

Setting the oil lamp down next to the stove, she pulled the kitchen nets aside and peered out into the night. The bleating had died down to an occasional terrified *baa*. Whatever had frightened the sheep was still out there. It was probably the same rustlers who had taken two cows from the Merryweather farm last month. Well, they weren't going to get any of *her* flock. She pulled on her overcoat and rain boots, grabbed her shotgun from the pantry, and filled her pockets with cartridges from the biscuit tin next to the tea bags.

The kitchen door clicked shut behind her as she stepped outside. Tucking the shotgun under her arm, she hitched up her nightie and crept through the orchard, silently weaving between the twisted plum trees toward the sheep pen. The new moon cast only a little light onto the farm, which was shrouded in the kind of darkness that makes it impossible to see your own feet. The dark didn't bother her. She didn't approve of the kind of skies where the glow of streetlights was always present and you couldn't see the stars. This was night as it should be.

The bleating had stopped and the sheep were eerily silent now. Nearing the pen, she could make out wet crunching noises punctuated with deep grunts.

Something was in with the sheep and it wasn't human. Could it be wolves? She hadn't heard of wolves in Hexbridge, not for many years.

Her eyes adjusted to the blackness, and she could just about make out a mass of sheep huddled together in one corner of the pen. The whole flock was constantly in motion as each animal clambered over the others, trying to get as far as possible from whatever was in there with them. Mrs. Emmett crept forward to investigate.

The crunching stopped and the frantic bleating started again as a huge, dark shape reared up between her and the pen. She had never heard sheep make noises like that before, not even in the slaughterhouse. Instinctively she raised the shotgun and fired two shots directly into the shadowy mass.

The recoil threw her to the ground and she was nearly deafened by a loud bellow, like an elephant and lion roaring at the same time. Tearing her nightie from the grip of the brambles, she clambered to her feet, only to reel back from the hot, stinking breath of the thing that towered above her.

She looked up.

Two pairs of yellow eyes as large as saucers glared down at her. The stench of sulfur filled her nostrils as the creatures began to hiss softly. As the noise became louder, she took a long deep breath. With amazing speed she reloaded, snapped the barrel shut, jammed the butt to her shoulder, and aimed right between the eyes of the closest creature. Squeezing the trigger, she shouted louder than she ever had in all her eighty-two years,

"SHOOOOO!"

The hammer clicked feebly as the gun failed to fire. The eyes seemed to half close into a smile as her mighty roar dwindled into silence. The hiss was now like a pressure cooker at full steam. A scorching gust of wind hit her, blowing off her nightcap and sending her hair and nightie billowing. With eyes closed tight, Mrs. Emmett shielded her face from the searing wind as a white-hot flash ended her worries about sheep forever. As the gun dropped from her hands, she just had time for one final entry on the list of things she disapproved of.

CHAPTER ONE

The Raven

As Alfie Bloom rocked back on his chair and enjoyed the lively chatter that filled the classroom, he had the strange sensation he was being watched.

It was the last day before summer vacation. The sun streamed through the windows, promising six weeks of glorious freedom, and Mrs. Harris had declared a free afternoon. Most of the pupils had brought in board games and were arguing loudly over who was winning and who was cheating. The arty students were drawing and painting pictures or scribbling ballpoint tattoos onto one another's arms.

Alfie had been happily daydreaming about nothing in particular when the feeling hit. It was beginning to irritate him. He glanced around the classroom suspiciously. Everyone seemed to be minding his or her own business, or one another's. He turned his attention to the playground, briefly catching his reflection in the window, a red-brown mop of hair falling across green eyes.

Gazing beyond, he realized who was spying on him. It was a large raven on the school field.

The raven gave a little hop, then strode from side to side, looking back at the classroom window over hunched shoulders. Alfie could swear that it was trying to act casual after being caught out. There wasn't another bird in sight, and he began to feel a little sorry for the solitary creature. Alfie knew what it was like to feel alone. The last day of the term always seemed so exciting, but tomorrow he would face being stuck on his own all summer while his best friend, Amy Sui, went on vacation with her gran. His dad was always so busy with his inventions and part-time jobs that Alfie knew he would hardly see him.

Forfeiting the staring contest, he stretched and turned to watch the card game at the next table. Amy seemed to be winning. Glancing back at the field, he froze. In place of the raven, a tall man in a Victorian suit and cape was looking directly at him through a small brass telescope. Alfie nearly fell off his chair.

"Amy! AMY!" he called, waving frantically at his friend. When he looked back at the field, the man had vanished and the raven was back.

"What's up, Al?" asked Amy, joining him. "This had better be good. I was just about to win Phil's pen—the one that writes in space."

"There! See that raven?" Alfie eyed the bird warily as it pecked nonchalantly at the feathers under its wing. "Does it look . . . *normal* to you?"

"Let's see." Amy leaned over his shoulder and gave the raven a good, hard squint. "Well, it's got all the usual bits—feathers, wings, beak—so yep, that's a normal bird all right. Is that all you called me for?"

"Yeah. Sorry." Alfie started to feel a little embarrassed. "It's just that . . . well, it looked *different* for a second."

"O-kaaay." Amy patted him on the head and went back to her game.

The classroom was still as noisy as ever. Mrs. Harris was trying to get everyone to put away their paints and games. No one else seemed to have noticed anything peculiar happening outside.

Alfie was still staring at the raven, wondering if he had just imagined the strange man, when the school bell sounded. Everyone jumped to their feet as a resounding cheer went around the classroom. He looked back at the field just in time to see the raven run a few steps before taking flight.

"Settle down, everyone," shouted Mrs. Harris. "Well, your grade-school years have come to an end. I hope that you all work hard at Hillston Middle School after summer vacation and that *some* of you take the opportunity of starting a new school to turn over a new leaf." Alfie noticed her glance at a couple of students in particular as she said this, but they were too busy inching closer to the door to take in the hint. "Please put your chairs on your tables QUIETLY and—" The rest was drowned out under the roar of chairs being dragged across the floor and plonked onto tables, some of them falling off as everyone shoved to get out of the door first. Mrs. Harris tried to shout a few more words of farewell over the din, then flopped into her chair with a sigh of relief that yet another year was over. Alfie pulled off his tie, slung his bag across his shoulders, and threw himself into the midst of the wild, whooping mob flowing out of the school.

He passed Amy just as she was getting into her gran's car.

"Gran says to come over on Sunday for lunch, Al. WOO! No more school!"

Alfie dallied more than usual on the way home, enjoying the raven mystery and the warm weather.

His daydreams ended abruptly as an empty Coke can hit the back of his head.

"Oi, Bloomers!"

Alfie groaned and mentally kicked himself. He had been too preoccupied to notice class troublemakers Vinnie and Weggis trailing along behind him.

"So, what you doing for summer vacation?" asked Vinnie as they caught up. "Is your weirdo dad taking you to dig up dinosaurs or something?"

"He's an inventor, not an archaeologist."

"Whatever, he's still a nutjob. Anyways, we thought we'd walk you home as we won't see you till September. Can't wait, though. I hear the toilets at Hillston flush for ages. Your hair could use a wash."

"Get lost," Alfie muttered under his breath, walking faster to leave them behind. Their insults and taunts about his dad had been chipping away at him for months, but he hadn't dared say a word back to them for fear of making things worse.

"What was that, Bloomers? Did you really just tell us to get lost? Get his bag, Weggis!"

Alfie tried to yank his bag away as Weggis lunged for it, but he was too slow.

Vinnie began rummaging through it, throwing out Alfie's gym clothes.

"Hmm, lame sneakers."

"They're okay." Weggis let go of Alfie and joined in.

"My dog'll 'ave 'em." He pulled out a workbook and flicked through it before tossing it aside and grabbing another.

Alfie sighed. He knew this routine—he'd seen it so many times in the playground. They would go through everything in his bag, then throw it to each other if he tried to take it back. He sat down on a garden wall and tried his hardest to look bored despite the blood pounding through his veins.

"Don't you want yer bag?" spat Weggis, clearly annoyed that Alfie wasn't making any effort to get it.

"You seem to want it more than me," said Alfie, hoping his voice wasn't shaking. He got up and began walking away. "Keep it."

"Oi, we don't want your stinking stuff!" shouted Vinnie, running over and shoving him in the back. Alfie stumbled forward, then spun around to face him. "At least we can afford decent sneakers." Vinnie slammed his palm into Alfie's shoulder this time. Alfie felt as though someone had lit a fire in his chest, and it was melting away his cold fear of Vinnie. "Bet your freak of a dad couldn't afford to buy another pair if you lost these." Alfie curled his fingers into fists. Another push.

Alfie snapped. He shoulder-charged the two boys,

catching them completely by surprise. The bag slipped out of Vinnie's hand as Weggis fell on top of him. It sailed over Alfie's head to land in the road. He raced to pick up his things before they untangled themselves to chase him.

His eyes felt hot and blurry as he grabbed his books and sneakers. He shoved them quickly into his bag while checking over his shoulder for Vinnie. A woman's voice called out sharply from behind him.

"Look out!"

He turned and froze on the spot. A car was speeding toward him. The driver spotted him and slammed on his brakes, but it was too late. Everything seemed to be moving in slow motion. The woman stood helplessly on the curb with her dog, her arm stretched out toward him. The car was so close Alfie could see the face of the driver in great detail—a middle-aged man with glasses and a moustache, his hands gripping the wheel as his mouth opened into a silent scream.

Unable to force his legs to move, Alfie closed his eyes and half crouched in terror, waiting for the impact as the car screeched toward him.

Then . . . nothing.

There was an eerie stillness. After a few seconds, he

realized that all sounds in the street had stopped. No voices, no birds, no traffic. The air felt different too: colder, with an earthy smell, like old leaves.

When he opened his eyes he was astonished to see that the street had gone, replaced by a cool grayish mist. The adrenaline flowed out of his veins as he uncurled. Why wasn't he hurting anywhere? His clothes were starting to feel damp. He held out his hand, and tiny droplets of rain splashed onto his palm. Could you get wet if you were dead?

A pigeon cooed somewhere above, breaking the stillness. The ground squelched under his feet as he stepped back to look up into the ghostly trees that surrounded him. Another noise cut through the air—a distant ax chopping wood. As he strained to hear more clearly, it began to fade along with the earthy smell and the mist. The familiar shapes and colors of the street began to reappear like colored paint spreading across wet paper.

Voices were shouting and a scream grew louder, as if someone was turning up the volume.

"Where did he go?"

"Is he under the car?"

Alfie blinked and looked around in surprise. He was back in the street at the side of the road. The car had stopped over the exact spot where he had been moments before. The driver was sitting with his hands on the wheel, shaking with shock.

"There he is!" cried the woman who had tried to warn him. She was staring in amazement, her dog barking wildly as it strained against its lead.

Barely able to believe he hadn't been hurt, Alfie slowly picked up his bag and began walking away. He passed the two bullies who were frozen like statues and picked up speed as they began to call after him. He wanted to get as far away as possible from whatever had just happened.

The blood started to pound in his ears as he broke into a run. By the time he turned into Abernathy Terrace, his side hurt and his breath was coming in gasps. The row of gray Victorian terraced houses seemed to stretch out for miles in front of him. His side hurt, but he kept running—past the house with the purple door, past gossipy Mrs. O'Riley's, past the tree he had fallen out of and broken his arm four years ago, past the window with the yappy white dog that always leapt up to bark at him.

As he ran he noticed a raven flying above him. Was it the same one? It swooped down to glide alongside Alfie as he tore down the street, then flapped its wings and soared up and away over the rooftops.

CHAPTER TWO

A Strange Invitation

A loud *boom* wrenched Alfie from dreams of ravens and misty forests. He sat up with a jolt, then relaxed as he realized it had come from his dad's workshop. He was probably working on something involving chemicals again. Alfie grimaced; the flat still smelled like burnt cabbage from the last time. His dad had invented dozens of almost useful devices—a water-powered hair dryer, a toilet-paper holder that sounded a deafening alarm when running low, and, most recently, a voice-activated front door that only seemed to understand Irish accents. None of these had made any money, so when Alfie's mum died two years ago, his dad had taken on a series of part-time jobs to make ends meet. The little spare time he had was divided between Alfie and his inventions. Alfie didn't care that they didn't have much money—he didn't even mind the dank basement flat too much. He just missed the way things used to be when his mum was alive.

Sitting up, he blinked groggily against the sun shining through his window. For a minute he wondered why he was wearing his school clothes, but then he remembered flopping onto his bed in exhaustion after racing home. He must have slept right through the evening and night. His dad had been working late again. Just as well. Alfie hadn't wanted to talk about his last day at school. He knew his dad had enough worries without hearing that Alfie had been getting into fights and was nearly hit by a car.

As he changed into scuffed jeans and a faded T-shirt, Alfie wondered what to do with the first day of summer vacation. The long, lonely weeks seemed to stretch out in front of him like a prison sentence. He wished his dad didn't have to work so hard. He wished Amy wasn't going on vacation. He wished his life wasn't so . . . so *dull*. Searching through his drawer for a pair of socks without holes in them, he wondered if he was the only kid in the world who hated school vacations.

A scratching noise broke through his brief moment of self-pity, alerting him to the arrival of a pale ginger tabby: Galileo. The cat nudged the door wide open and padded into the room purring. Alfie reached down to scratch behind his ears and noticed the cat was carrying something in his mouth. An envelope. Galileo dropped it on the threadbare rug, then flopped down next to a pair of shoes and began lazily chewing the laces.

"Weirdo," Alfie laughed. "Are you training to be a dog?"

He picked up the expensive-looking envelope. On the front, in beautifully neat handwriting, were the words:

For the attention of Alfred Bloom

He made a face. Only people like his headmaster, the landlady, or angry old Mr. Filbert upstairs assumed his name should be lengthened to Alfred. On the back was a large wax seal with two ravens perched on a pair of scales. He thought it a shame to break it, but within seconds it was lying in pieces and he was holding an official-looking letter. Alfie took a deep sniff of the thick cream paper—it smelled like old books. It was embossed with a gold crest that matched the seal and read:

Muninn and Bone Solicitors (Established 1086)

Dear Master Bloom,

An appointment has been arranged for you with one of our senior partners on Saturday 23rd July at 11:59 p.m. to discuss the transference of your substantial inheritance.

We are legally required to also request the presence of your father, Mr. William Horatio Bloom.

Our carriage will call for you at 11:26 p.m. prompt.

Sincerely,
Emily Fortune
Senior Administrator

Substantial inheritance? Had someone left him something in a will? Alfie read the card again, his head spinning. It was the twenty-third today. He raced to his dad's workshop with the strange invitation.

"You're absolutely sure it isn't someone from school playing a joke on you?" said his dad as he read through the letter at the rickety kitchen table, scratching the back of his neck thoughtfully.

"Yes, I'm sure, Dad, for the fifth time!" Alfie mumbled through a mouthful of tuna, sprout, and pickled-egg sandwich. Breakfast was often a creative mix of whatever was left in the cupboards. "I don't know anyone who could forge something that well."

Alfie's dad was a tall man with dark hair that tended to stick out all over the place. Alfie thought it was most probably because he spent so much time scratching his head. He was wearing his favorite cardigan—the green one with lots of pockets that his mum had knitted. Alfie noticed it was a lot baggier on him than it used to be. He risked another sandwich as he waited impatiently for his dad to finish analyzing the letter. This one contained chips, beets, and pickles. At long last his dad got up.

"Cup of tea, son?" He rummaged around in the murky green cupboards above the sink for tea bags and clean cups. Mrs. Craddock, the landlady, hadn't decorated the flat for about forty years. They had moved here a few years ago to save money to build their own house, but since Alfie's mum died, their savings had dwindled away. His dad didn't talk about building a house anymore. Alfie understood why—even if they could afford it, he didn't want to live in Mum's dream house without her either.

"Well, Alfie," he said as he poured the tea. "I've never heard of this Muninn and Bone, but I have to admit, the letter does look genuine."

"What do you think they mean by *substantial inheritance*?" asked Alfie. No one they knew had died—not recently—and they didn't know anyone even remotely rich.

"I guess there's only one way to find out." His dad smiled and passed him one of the steaming cups.

At quarter past eleven, Alfie and his dad were already sitting on the wall outside their basement flat on Abernathy Terrace. It was a warm summer night and the scent of jasmine from the garden next door filled the air. The sweet smell began to give Alfie a headache as he sat uncomfortably straight, trying not to crease his clothes. They had spent the afternoon scouring charity shops for smart clothes. Alfie was quite pleased with his dark gray suit, but had to fasten his belt very tightly to stop the trousers dropping down around his ankles. He had managed to talk his dad out of buying a plaid blazer and into getting something quite smart and sensible, although the effect was rather spoiled by slightly short trousers, which showed his odd socks.

The minute hand on his watch drew nearer to 11:26. Alfie looked up and down the street anxiously. He began to feel silly. Maybe the letter really was a joke. What kind of lawyer would want to meet at midnight? Just as he was about to suggest they go back inside, there was a clatter of hooves on the street. He nearly toppled back over the wall in shock when he saw what was standing there.

Smack bang in front of him stood the grandest coach imaginable—bigger and better than all those in the Tower of London put together. The varnished ebony wood was so highly polished that it could have been mistaken for glass. Even the ornately framed windows were black. A shiny silver cap bearing the same crest as the invitation sat at the center of each wheel. He looked up to see a man in a top hat and traveling cape sitting high at the front. The man held the reins to six huge black horses, which snorted and stamped the ground impatiently. Alfie couldn't believe he hadn't heard their approach before the sudden clatter.

The driver tipped his hat. "Johannes." He was a giant of a man with neat gray-flecked sideburns that framed his good-humored face, and he introduced himself in a gravelly voice with a hint of a German accent before nodding toward the coach door. It opened and two steps slid out of the frame. "Please take your seats, sirs." Alfie felt a shiver of excitement as they climbed inside the coach and settled into the luxurious purple velvet seats.

"Fasten your seat belts." Alfie jumped as the driver's voice boomed through a brass funnel on the wall in front of them. "The boiled sweets provided will ease any discomfort you feel in your ears during the journey."

Alfie gingerly helped himself to a sweet from a silver dish fixed to the wall as his dad admired the plush interior of the carriage. "I've never been in anything this fancy in my entire life," he whispered as though half afraid the driver was listening to them. "Whatever they want to speak to you about must be very important."

The steps folded back into a small compartment with a quiet whirring noise, and the door closed, making barely a sound. With a tiny jerk, they were on their way.

Alfie could hear the horses snorting and the coachman half singing, half shouting to them as they galloped.

"Dad," said Alfie. "We must be going very fast. You don't think we'll crash, do you?"

"I'm sure the driver knows what he's doing," said his dad, although he didn't look entirely convinced.

The coach began to travel faster and faster until Alfie

was sitting right back in his seat, hands gripping the silver handles on the walls as he glanced worriedly at his dad. There was a sudden jolt and everything tilted backward. Alfie felt as though an invisible hippopotamus was sitting on him. The feeling lasted for about a minute before the pressure eased, the carriage stopped shuddering, and he could move freely again.

"Whoa! That was weird," he exclaimed, swallowing to pop his ears while gathering up the sweets that had slid into his lap.

"It gets stranger," said his dad, sitting up and leaning his head toward the window. "Listen carefully. Tell me what you hear."

Alfie strained to hear anything. "Nothing. Just a whistling noise."

"Exactly. Why can't we hear the horses galloping anymore?" Alfie stared at his dad. Surely they couldn't be . . . flying?

Alfie pushed his face to the window, cupping his hands around his eyes like binoculars. It was dark outside and the thick, tinted glass made everything even darker. He could just about make out flashes of color and light. He spent much of the journey grinning at his dad, who beamed back at him as though too full of anticipation to even talk. Alfie felt as though they were on a marvelous adventure together, and he wrapped his arms around his stomach to try to trap the warm feeling it gave him inside.

After about twenty minutes, the whole coach jarred with a loud thud. Alfie grabbed his seat again as they were bounced up and down. The whistling had stopped and he could hear the sharp sound of horses' hooves slowing to a trot as the coach rolled to a halt.

The door opened with a *pop*, and Alfie nearly fell out face-first. His dad caught his arm as he half jumped, half toppled to the cobbles below. They were in an old coach house the size of a warehouse with vast oak doors that were now closed.

Steam rose from the horses as the driver placed a barrel of water in front of each one. He spoke to them gently in a horsey language full of neighs, nickers, and snorts. In the dim light cast by the flickering torches on the walls, Alfie could see coaches of all shapes and sizes. He ran over to an enormous one that looked like a golden barge from Ancient Egypt, but with wheels.

"Look at this, Dad!" he shouted as he discovered a green-and-gold coach half his height and peered through the tiny windows. *Surely no one could fit into something so small.*

"It must be a toy." His dad squatted down for a closer

look. "Look at these tiny symbols around the sides." He adjusted his glasses and leaned forward for a closer look.

"Ahem!" A huge hand landed on each of their shoulders, and Alfie looked up to see Johannes towering over them. "This way, sirs. Mr. Bone is waiting."

He led them to a gigantic door made up of lots of other doors of decreasing size, one inside the other, like Russian nesting dolls. The smallest only came halfway up Alfie's knee. "Just through there. Ms. Fortune will sign you in."

"Which door do we open?"

The coachman chuckled as he filled a nose bag for each horse. "Whichever one fits, Master Bloom, whichever one fits."

Alfie stared in awe as he swung the human-sized door open to reveal a magnificent round room. The floor was made of marble with the now familiar Muninn and Bone crest set into a disk of polished brass in the center. The walls were covered in dark wooden panels and the stone arched ceiling was so high that he felt as if he were in a cathedral. At least twenty suits of armor in all shapes and sizes lined the paneled walls.

"Mister and Master Bloom?" said a bright little voice from behind them. "How do you do?"

Alfie spun around in surprise. They had walked

straight past a young woman behind the huge desk near the entrance. Her long dark hair flowed out behind her as she skipped over to shake hands.

"I'm sorry, we didn't see you!" he stammered.

"Not a problem, not a problem at all. Everyone reacts like that when they first come here." She spun on the spot with her arms outstretched. "Such a grand old hall and such a little old me."

Alfie liked this tiny woman with her singsong voice, huge green eyes, and pointy face. "You're not old," he said, unable to keep from blushing.

"Maybe I am, maybe I'm not. It all depends on how you look at it." She smiled. "I think I'm going to like you a whole bunch, Master Bloom. Now wherever did I leave my manners? I'm Emily—Emily Fortune—originally Amelia Fortuna, but that sounds far too much like a frumpy old fish, so I tweaked the first name and swapped an A for an E. Much more modern now, isn't it? Very classy, very sassy, very *now*! One should always keep up with the times, don't you think?" Alfie didn't have time to reply as she ushered them over to her desk. "Anyhoo, chop-chop, let's get you signed in before you head on up to your meeting. If you like this room, just wait until you see Mr. Bone's office. *Very* swish."

Alfie finally exhaled as Emily finished talking and

plonked a large book in front of them. He took a deep breath and noticed his dad do the same. He wondered how she found time to breathe.

"Okay, just press your thumbs on this ink pad for me . . . good, now stick your thumbprint next to your name and the time . . . thank you. Now, if you could both shimmy onto the crest, please."

Alfie wasn't quite sure how to shimmy but followed his dad and stepped onto the brass disk in the center of the room.

"Lovely, thank you. Now hold still and keep your feet away from the edges. This won't hurt a bit, and you'll be there in a jiffy."

"Wait, what's going to happen?" asked Alfie apprehensively as he noticed a long brass cylinder descending from the ceiling like a telescope extending. "Ms. Fortune?"

"Don't worry, it's perfectly safe," she assured them. "Well, as long as you don't touch the sides . . ."

CHAPTER THREE

Caspian Bone

Everything went black as the cylinder dropped down over them. With a *click* and a *whoosh*, the crest beneath their feet propelled them upward at a startling rate. Beyond the brass cylinder that had descended from the ceiling, the walls were stone, worn smooth as marble by the disk's passage. Alfie fought the urge to touch them as they whizzed by and stayed as close to the center of the crest as he could. Light flickered into the elevator as door after door with porthole-style windows zoomed by. Alfie thought that it was the best elevator he had ever traveled in and tried to glimpse whatever was through the little windows as they flew past.

"What an ingenious system!" In the flickering light Alfie could see that his dad was grinning from ear to ear. "Do you hear that whooshing noise? I'll bet the disk we are standing on is being propelled upward by air alone. The pressure required to lift both it and us must be immense." Alfie smiled. His dad was always happiest when trying to figure out how something worked. "Hmm, something would be needed to stop us at the right floor—there must be a powerful clamp on each level. It would need to grab the edge of this disk at exactly the right millisecond to stop us shooting through the roof."

He was proved right when the disk stopped moving with a loud clank in front of a brass door. As their feet landed back on the floor, he laughed with delight and patted the wall.

"Remarkable."

The door slid open. Alfie stared in awe as they stepped into an enormous round room with a beautiful blue domed ceiling onto which constellations of stars had been painted. A winged device made of wood and canvas hung from the center. He recognized it from a picture in his dad's favorite book on Leonardo da Vinci.

"Alfred and William Bloom, I presume?"

A tall, dignified figure had risen from a deep leather armchair in front of a fire that burned with a green flame.

"It's just Alfie, not Alfred," Alfie replied before he could stop himself.

"I will ensure that our records are amended accordingly," said the man in a crisp tone. "Now, if I may introduce myself, I am Caspian Bone, senior partner at this firm. I have been expecting this meeting for longer than you might imagine."

Alfie took in Caspian Bone's quirky appearance as he shook his hand. His sharp, pale face was framed by shining shoulder-length ebony hair. The irises of his eyes were almost completely black. He didn't look much older than his mid-thirties, but wore an old-fashioned, tailored black suit, giving him the appearance of a Victorian gentleman. Alfie's gaze shifted to the cape hanging on a coat stand and something clicked in his memory.

"It's you!" he shouted triumphantly. "You're real! You were watching me yesterday from the school field. You turned into a bird, then later, after the car . . ."

"Perhaps so," said the lawyer. His head twitched to one side as he stared intently at Alfie. "However, tonight we deal solely with your inheritance and matters pertaining to it."

"Has someone died?" Alfie barely heard his dad ask the question as he stared up at the lawyer, wondering what he really was and why he had been spying on him.

"The inheritance we are here to discuss is not related to the recent demise of any friends, family, or acquaintances. It is the legacy of Orin Hopcraft."

"Orin Hopcraft!" whispered Alfie's dad, reeling back slightly. "So he *was* real?"

Alfie was surprised at his dad's reaction to the strange name. Who were they talking about?

"If you would both take a seat." Caspian led the way to his stately desk and Alfie found himself dropping obediently into one of the chairs offered.

"Now, to business." Caspian reached into a drawer and produced a large leather binder, which he laid on the desk between them. He sat forward, gazing down his long sharp nose at Alfie, his fingers steepled in front of his chest.

"At four in the afternoon, on the twenty-second of July, you performed an unaided timeslip."

Alfie snapped his attention away from the binder and looked at the lawyer accusingly. "Wait, I did *what*?" That was the time he would have been walking home from school.

"Alfie timeslipped on his own?" gasped his dad. "Is this because of where he was born?"

"Indeed," said the lawyer.

Alfie couldn't believe what he was hearing. Caspian was clearly crazy. Looking up at his father's flushed face, he was even more shocked to see that he wasn't surprised by the lawyer's words. "Dad, what is he talking about, and who is Orin Hopcraft?"

"My apologies," said Caspian, looking from Alfie to his dad. "I was unaware that your father had not revealed the unusual circumstances surrounding your birth."

Alfie's dad shifted uncomfortably on his chair. "It hardly seemed real," he mumbled, trying to avoid Alfie's gaze. "His mum wanted him to hear about it where it happened, and we just never got around to telling him . . ."

"Telling me what?" asked Alfie, using all of his reserve to stop himself kicking Caspian's desk in frustration.

"I'm afraid that conversation is between you and your father," interrupted Caspian. "At present, we have other matters to discuss."

Alfie didn't feel remotely ready to let the matter drop, but the lawyer's unblinking stare and authoritative tone won the battle. Alfie sank back in his chair as Caspian pushed the leather binder across the desk toward him, looking even more like a raven now as his hair glinted with blues and purples under the light of the oil lamps. Alfie opened the file. It contained a bundle of documents written in elegant calligraphy on parchment that was slightly brown and curled around the edges.

"These deeds were entrusted to this firm quite some time ago with the instruction that they pass to you on your twelfth birthday. However, in light of yesterday's . . . *event*, we deemed it necessary to set into motion the early transference of your inheritance."

Alfie scanned the pages of legal text and a familiar name caught his eye. A name linked to the village where his mum's family still lived. He looked up in amazement. "These papers . . . they're about Hexbridge Castle?"

"Your castle," asserted Caspian.

"You're kidding?" Alfie searched Caspian's face for the slightest sign that this was a joke. He found none.

"I do not kid. The deeds are yours, making the castle yours."

Alfie clutched the papers to his chest as if they might blow away at any second.

"Seriously? I can live in it if I want?"

"That is, in fact, the only caveat. You *must* live in it. It contains a great deal of Orin's work and most precious possessions, and they are to pass only to you and your heirs. The castle can never be sold or pass out of your family. If you cease to call it your home, it will seal itself forever."

"How can Alfie own a castle? He's only eleven!"

"I'm nearly twelve, Dad," said Alfie, already imagining life in Hexbridge Castle near the farm where his cousins, Madeleine and Robin, lived. He could visit them every day!

"As you know, the castle has been sealed for hundreds of years," Caspian continued, "although it is still in the same fine condition as the day it was left. I assumed that you would require certain aspects of the building to be brought up to modern standards and have taken the liberty of arranging the renovation. The work will be conducted over the next four days, after which time you will move into your new home."

Alfie noted the way that Caspian spat out the word "modern" as though it had left an unpleasant taste in his mouth.

"That must be an awful lot of work," said his dad. "Can it really be done in so little time? Surely it would take weeks."

"With our contractors, anything is possible," replied the lawyer. "I will meet you outside the castle at noon in four days' time to hand over the keys."

"Wait a minute, Mr. Bone." Alfie's dad looked as though he had just snapped out of a dream. "You're assuming too much. Don't we have any say in this? I can't afford the upkeep on a building like that. What about the bills?"

Caspian looked mildly amused. "You will find the castle remarkably self-sustaining. As Alfie's guardian, you inherit a generous monthly allowance that will be transferred into Alfie's name when he comes of age. It will provide very well for both your needs."

"That may be so, but this all sounds far too good to be true. What's the catch, Mr. Bone?"

"No catch. Take it, or leave it."

Alfie stared incredulously at his dad as Caspian tapped his fingers impatiently on his desk. "Are you kidding? We can live in a castle instead of our poxy old flat! You won't have to worry about working all those jobs."

"I know, Alfie, but just think about the practicalities."

"You'll have a lot more room to work on your inventions." Alfie couldn't believe he had to convince his dad to accept a free castle. "You're always saying the workshop is too small. Imagine what you could create with all that space to work in."

His father gazed up at the flying machine hanging from the ceiling. Alfie sensed him weakening and began to list all of the projects he would be able to finish.

"Okay, okay," he sighed finally. "But this is all happening very fast. I'd like to think I had *some* choice in it."

"I apologize if I seemed presumptuous," said Caspian Bone, looking at his fingernails and not appearing the slightest bit sorry. "However, the choice is Alfie's to make, and I believe he has already decided."

Alfie beamed at his dad, who laughed and threw up his hands in defeat.

"If I may continue?" Caspian flipped through pages that Alfie could have sworn were blank seconds before. "As you can see, the name on the deed now reads Alfie Bloom. These should be kept somewhere secure. I suggest that you continue to entrust them to our care."

"That's fine by me," said Alfie. After the strange journey, he had the feeling that Muninn and Bone was a very safe and secret place indeed.

"A wise decision, Master Bloom. They will be transferred back to the vaults. Now, the final matter on the agenda." Caspian drew a small velvet pouch from his breast pocket and placed it into Alfie's hand. "Open it."

Alfie reached inside and pulled out a thin gold disk the size of a two-pound coin. There was a strip of leather threaded through a loop at the top so that it could be worn around the neck. Lots of tiny runic symbols had been scratched into the gold, spiraling out from a purple-colored lens in the center. It felt warm in his fingers and looked old. Very old.

"What is it?" he asked.

"An ocular talisman," replied Caspian, as though the answer was obvious. "Put it on."

"A *what* talisman?"

"Ocular. It means you can look through it. Make sure you wear it at all times."

"Why?" asked Alfie as he fastened the cord around his neck.

"Please excuse me." Caspian stood up and straightened his jacket.

"But, I wanted to ask—" began Alfie.

"Our business is concluded. I have matters to attend to elsewhere." Caspian stepped around the desk and shook their hands again. "Congratulations on your marvelous inheritance. Our next meeting will be at your new residence."

Alfie and his dad stood up, still reeling at the news and rather surprised at the abrupt end to the meeting.

"Aren't you traveling down with us, Mr. Bone?" asked Alfie as they were ushered back onto the brass disk.

"I will use the other exit," replied Caspian.

Alfie's eye fell on a large open window, and Caspian gave him the tiniest hint of a nod before the door slid shut.

Thankfully the elevator was slower on the way down.

Emily Fortune met them at the bottom, and they signed the book to confirm the time they had left. Alfie had slightly longer to look at it this time and noticed how strange some of the other thumbprints were. Next to two names that could only have been read with a magnifying glass were two tiny handprints. Then there was a thumbprint as big as a fist next to a huge scrawled signature. The other three visitors that day had written their names in hieroglyphics, and there was a little prick mark above each of their prints, as if the owners had claws.

"Ooh, I see you're wearing Orin's talisman," said Emily as she closed the book. "Very good, but Mr. Bone should have told you to keep it hidden. You may meet people who shouldn't discover that you have something like that."

"Do you know what it is and why I have to wear it?"

"You mean no one has explained it to you yet?"

"No one has explained *anything*!"

"Oh dear. Mr. Bone does love to make things mysterious."

"He's not the only one." Alfie cast a sideways look at his dad, who suddenly appeared very interested in the ceiling.

"May I?" She knelt down and held the disk. Alfie noticed that her fingers were adorned with beautiful, delicate silver rings. "It is many things: a key to at least one door that should never be opened and a lens that can reveal secrets and focus energy. It is also a protective talisman. A very valuable gift from Orin Hopcraft."

"Caspian kept saying that name. Who is he?"

"The Great Druid. The last time I saw him was right here in this office many years ago. You met him too, on the day you were born. This talisman was to be a gift on your twelfth birthday. As you're moving to the castle now, we thought you should start wearing it early, just in case."

"In case of what?"

Emily tucked the talisman into his shirt and patted his shoulder. "I don't mean to scare you, but better safe than sad. Or is it sorry? I forget. You'll have a wonderful time exploring the castle—it has been empty for so long." She handed Alfie a folder. "I put together some news clippings about it and made copies of the plans for you. I'm sure there are plenty of wonderful things that aren't marked, but at least you can decide which bedroom is going to be yours."

Alfie took the folder and hugged it tightly to his chest, visions of thrones, dungeons, and secret passages swimming through his head.

"Right, busy-busy. Sorry to chase you, things to do, people to see."

"Ms. Fortune, can you tell us where we are?" asked Alfie as Emily placed a dainty hand on each of their backs and hustled them through the door. He had been puzzling over the lack of address on the appointment letter, and the journey had been pretty weird, to say the least.

"Ah, now I need to be as mysterious as Mr. Bone. The whereabouts of our offices must remain forever secret due to the nature of the items we hold. There is nowhere more secure than here, but that doesn't mean we should advertise our location. Now, take care, I'm sure we'll meet again, and please, call me Emily."

With that she gave a little wave and closed the door, leaving them back in the coach house, where the carriage waited to take them home.

CHAPTER FOUR

The Hexbridge Rustlers

The next couple of days were spent in a flurry of activity. Aunt Grace had insisted they move to Hexbridge immediately when Alfie's dad called to tell her the news. She had invited them to stay on the farm until the castle was ready. Alfie could hardly wait. He bundled his meager possessions into boxes in no time and then started helping to dismantle and pack his dad's devices. He didn't know what half of them actually did and had a sneaking suspicion his dad wasn't sure either.

As they packed, he couldn't keep his mind off the mysteries surrounding the move. His life had taken a very strange turn over the last few days. He almost expected to be told that it was a mistake and that Emily had contacted the wrong Alfie Bloom. He kept trying to pressure his dad into telling him about Orin Hopcraft and why a stranger would leave him a castle, but he remained frustratingly tight-lipped, promising to reveal all once they were in Hexbridge Castle. Alfie couldn't understand why he was being so secretive. What on earth had happened on the day he was born?

Mrs. Craddock, the landlady, had waived the three-month notice period, and Alfie thought she seemed relieved they were leaving. He suspected it had something to do with all the explosions she must have heard from the flat. Finally, when everything was neatly boxed and labeled, he escaped to visit Amy.

"Alfie Bloom, king of his own castle." Amy shook her head incredulously for the fifth time as she took a swig from her bottle of Coke. "Crazy."

Amy lived with her gran in the flat above her tea shop. Her parents had disappeared without a trace on a trip to Edinburgh when she was just five years old. When Alfie's mum died, the other children didn't seem to know what to say and avoided talking to him. Amy was the only person to understand how he felt. He would have been alone at school if it weren't for her.

Alfie had filled her in on everything that had happened since school while they munched on cakes in the tea shop. Hardly anything ever surprised Amy, so he was delighted to see her speechless for once.

"Don't you dare start thinking you can lord it over

me now, Your Majesty," she warned Alfie as his dad arrived to pick him up in his wood-framed green Morris Minor.

"I wouldn't dream of it, peasant," grinned Alfie as he climbed into the overloaded car and carefully balanced Galileo's travel cage on his knees. "Promise you'll visit as soon as you can?"

"Promise!" Amy reached her fist through the car window and they bumped knuckles. "Take care of yourself, Al."

"You too, Siu."

Alfie waved to Amy all the way down the street, trying to swallow the large lump that suddenly filled his throat as he left his best friend behind.

"Say good-bye to the flat!" shouted his dad as they drove down Abernathy Terrace for the last time. Alfie waved good-bye. Good-bye to the moldy little flat, good-bye to the city, good-bye to his boring old life. His heart soared. It was as though he was waking up to find that an amazing dream had come true.

Alfie spent the first half of the four-hour drive trying to get his dad to tell him how someone who must have died hundreds of years ago could have left him a castle. When that failed, they spent the rest of the journey playing guessing games. Alfie couldn't remember the last time he had spent so long talking with his dad. Finally, he began to see the first signs for Hexbridge and counted down the miles as they drew closer and closer.

"There it is, Alfie," said his dad at last. "Our new home."

Alfie looked out the car window to see Hexbridge Castle, *his* castle, sitting on the edge of a cliff that dropped down to Lake Archelon below. It was incredible. It looked as though someone had taken the best bits of lots of other castles and squished them together into one compact structure with towers, turrets, balconies, and battlements galore. A small, fast-moving river flowed down from higher in the hills, circling the castle before cascading off the cliff at either side as two sparkling waterfalls. Alfie stared breathlessly. It was the most beautiful thing he had ever seen. If only he didn't have to wait two whole nights before moving in.

He finally tore his eyes away as they turned into the leafy, sun-dappled lane that led toward the Merryweather farm, where his mum and Uncle Herb had grown up. As they turned through an almost invisible gap in the hedgerows, two children yelled with delight and leapt off the gate they were sitting on. The girl had dark blonde hair that looked as though it hadn't seen a brush in days. The boy's hair was the same color but considerably neater, as were his clothes. Alfie smiled. It always amazed him that his cousins looked so similar, yet so unalike at the same time.

"Alfie!" they shouted, swinging the gate wide open and running alongside the car as it trundled up the lane toward the farmhouse.

"We thought you'd *never* get here!"

"Mum said you're going to live in the castle," yelled Madeleine through the window, her hair streaming out behind her. "Who gave it to you? Are you rich now?"

Before he had time to answer, Robin joined in through the other window, his eyes shining.

"Can we explore it with you? All the castles I've been to are in ruins. It'll be brilliant to see inside one that has been locked up for centuries."

Alfie laughed to see his cousin's usually serious face lit up with excitement.

"I want to see the dungeons," added Madeleine, wrenching the door open to pull Alfie out before the car had even rolled to a stop. "I bet there'll be torture devices down there!"

"For goodness' sake, leave the poor boy alone," called a voice. "He's been traveling all day and I'm sure he'd like something to eat before you start pestering him."

"Aunt Grace!" yelled Alfie as a woman with wild curly hair bustled out of the farmhouse toward them. Before he knew it, he had been swept up into a hug so tight he could hardly breathe.

"Hmm, a bit pale and skinny," she said as she looked him up and down appraisingly. "But nothing fresh air and good food won't put right! And you, William Horatio Bloom!" Aunt Grace spun around to inspect Alfie's dad as he lifted Galileo's cat carrier from the car. "We really need to get some meat on those bird bones of yours. Why haven't you been to see us for so long?"

They were ushered into the kitchen, where the twins were setting the table. Alfie just had time to realize how hungry he was before a small woman with pure white hair and mischievous eyes rushed over to plant big kisses on both his cheeks. The familiar scent of violet cologne and peppermints wafted around him—he could never smell either of those things without thinking of Granny Merryweather.

"My little Alfie! Look at you, taller than me now. Remember to stop growing when you're tall enough— my Herb forgot and now he has to duck through doors."

"Dad's sorry he's not here," said Madeleine, pouring the juice as Alfie was pushed into a seat at the kitchen table. "He's gone to the cattle auction in Muggridge to replace some cows and won't be back till late."

"Come on, eat up," encouraged Granny. "Gracie has made a smashing crumble for dessert and you two look as though you haven't eaten in weeks."

Alfie was glad he was so hungry; he could swear the table was groaning louder than his stomach under the weight of the food. His mouth watered as he saw three types of freshly baked pie, soda bread hot from the oven, buttery new potatoes, and a golden roast chicken surrounded by crisp lettuce and tomatoes fresh from the garden. Between the mountain of food and the twins' never-ending questions about the castle, dinner lasted a very long time.

Finally, when no one could eat any more, Aunt Grace swept the plates away and suggested that Alfie and the twins walk Granny home while the adults cleared up and unpacked the car. He didn't need much convincing to get out of doing dishes.

Granny linked his arm as they walked down the lane while Madeleine darted around searching for rabbits hiding in the overgrown ditches.

"Why does Uncle Herb need to replace cows? Did he lose some?"

"Animals are always going missing round here," called Madeleine, grabbing at a frog that kept slipping through her fingers. "For as long as anyone can remember."

"It's true," said Granny. "Old Ernie Wilmslow says that even his great-granddad lost a few animals every year. Always on a new moon too, when it's darkest. I think rustling has become someone's family business."

"Dad said when he was a kid, he would sneak out with Auntie Jenny to set traps for them," Robin chimed in. "They never saw anyone though."

"Your grandpa put a stop to it in the end," said Granny. "He got tired of nets dropping over him whenever he went into the cattle shed."

Alfie tried to imagine his mum and uncle as mischievous children but couldn't picture Uncle Herb ever being young. On the way back to the farmhouse, a brilliant idea hit him.

"Hey, why don't we have a stakeout? Maybe we could catch the rustlers ourselves. Wouldn't that be the best adventure for summer vacation?"

Madeleine's face lit up at the mention of adventure.

"I can't believe we never thought of it. There's no way Dad can say no if he did it himself!"

By the time they got back to the farmhouse their minds were set.

"I'll work out when the next few new moons are," said Robin as he headed up to bed. "We need to plan carefully though. This could be dangerous."

Madeleine rolled her eyes at Alfie as she disappeared into her bedroom.

It took Alfie a second to remember where he was when he woke up in the top bunk of Robin's bed. He blinked his eyes against the morning sun as he sat up and knocked his head on a wooden airship hanging from the ceiling. The walls were covered with star charts, diagrams of insects, and posters of dinosaurs. Robin was sitting at his desk, scribbling in a little notebook as he studied the ant farm in front of him.

"Morning, cuz." Alfie climbed down from the bed and peered through the large telescope in front of the window. "I see you're still interested in, well, absolutely everything!"

Robin laughed. "Maddie reckons there isn't enough room in my brain for everything I want to know."

"Only because it's so small you'd need that microscope to find it," said Madeleine, sticking her head around the door.

"It's a telescope, not a microscope, genius." Robin spun the telescope around and pointed it at Madeleine's ear. "Hey, Alfie, look, you can see straight through!"

"Idiot!"

Alfie ducked as Madeleine slapped the telescope and sent it spinning.

"Anyway, get moving. We've loads to do and Dad wants to see Alfie before we go."

Alfie spent the whole day adventuring with the twins. He had forgotten just how much he loved spending time with them. While Robin was neat and tidy and seemed to know everything about everything, Madeleine's knees and elbows were always covered in scrapes and scabs, each of which had a great story behind it—even if it wasn't always quite the truth.

After an exhausting day spent exploring the woods, apple picking, skipping stones in Lake Archelon, and playing pirates in the twin's rickety tree house, Alfie was ravenous. When Aunt Grace called them in for dinner, he raced his cousins to the kitchen.

A moving van had dropped the full contents of their flat off that afternoon, but with all of his devices still boxed up, Alfie's dad had spent the whole day working on the farm with Uncle Herb. Alfie had to nudge him several times during dinner to stop him falling asleep in his stew and dumplings.

"Hold on a minute!" called Aunt Grace as Alfie and the twins finished their dinner and tried to slip off to play board games.

"I know—dishes!" said Robin as they trooped back into the kitchen.

"Good guess, but not this time," said Aunt Grace, holding out a shopping bag full of jams and pickles. "I want all of you to take these over to Mrs. Emmett and apologize for stealing her apples."

Alfie's heart sank when he realized whose apples they had picked and eaten that morning. He tried to slide behind the twins as they pulled their best innocent faces.

"Yes, don't think I didn't see you in her trees, and if I saw you, Mrs. Emmett did too. So get over there and apologize before she comes knocking. I'll be checking that you did!"

"Aww, they weren't even ripe anyway," groaned Madeleine as they traipsed out of the house.

"Tell her I found three of her sheep in our fields yesterday," Uncle Herb called after them. "They seem a bit jumpy, so I'll bring them over in the morning if they've calmed down."

"Fine," said Madeleine gloomily, before muttering under her breath, "So why don't *you* take the jam over tomorrow?"

"What was that?" Uncle Herb called from the kitchen.

"Nothing!"

Alfie's stomach continued to squirm as they trekked down the lane to the neighboring farm. He had met Mrs. Emmett on previous visits, and most of his memories were of her chasing him for one reason or another. Once she even chased him out of the post office for opening the door for her. She had shouted down the street asking if he thought she was too feeble to open it herself.

It was still quite light when they reached Mrs. Emmett's house. Alfie had always been nervous about going anywhere near it, as though she would run out and chase him at any minute. As they crept through the orchard, he could see that his cousins were just as wary. It was the creepiest-looking orchard Alfie had ever seen. The trees were bent over like scary old witches reaching out to grab him with their long, gnarly fingers.

"*You* knock," said Madeleine, nudging Robin forward as they reached the house.

"No way, it was your idea to pick the apples!" said Robin, slipping back behind her.

"Yeah, but I knocked last time."

"It was your idea *that* time too!"

Alfie knew this could go on for hours, and he wanted to get off Mrs. Emmett's land as soon as possible.

"I'll do it," he sighed, finally. He tapped lightly three times, holding his breath to listen for sounds from the house as he waited a whole long minute. No answer. Robin and Madeleine nudged him forward again as they cowered behind him. Alfie was sure the trees were watching him as he reached out and rapped harder. Madeleine gave a nervous squeak as the door swung open under his touch.

Nerves jangling, Alfie stuck his head into the musty old kitchen. "Mrs. Emmett—are you there?" He stepped back a little, ready to run if the old lady appeared. Something didn't feel right. "She's definitely not home," he whispered at last.

"Great," said Madeleine, brightening considerably. "We can just leave these and head back."

"Hold on, Maddie. Can you see Mrs. Emmett leaving her door unlocked for even a minute?" said Robin.

"That means she'll be back soon, so let's scoot!" Madeleine dumped the bag just inside the door and darted back outside.

Alfie had a gnawing feeling in his chest. He crossed the kitchen and touched the stove. It was cold, as though it hadn't been lit all day. An empty oil lamp sat on the counter nearby. It looked as though it had been left to burn itself out. Spotting the open tin of shotgun cartridges next to the kettle, he held one out to the twins. "Something's very wrong."

"The sheep on our farm!" gasped Robin. "It was a new moon four nights ago. Maybe she heard the rustlers and went out to confront them."

Alfie ran outside and scanned the fields. "Look, the sheep pen!"

Only one side of the pen was left standing; the rest was broken to pieces, as though it had been stomped by a giant. They rushed toward it and were greeted by a grisly sight. The wood scattered across the pen was stained with blood.

Alfie nudged a piece of wood with his foot and leapt back in horror as it slid away to reveal a bloodied hoof.

"This doesn't make sense. Why would rustlers kill the animals they were stealing?"

"They wouldn't." Robin prodded the hoof with a

stick. "They must have needed a truck to put the sheep in. Maybe they crashed through the fence and accidentally killed one."

Alfie couldn't see any tire tracks. He wished they'd gone home when Mrs. Emmett didn't answer the door. Something very bad had happened here.

"Come and look at this," called Madeleine.

She was staring at a pile of ashes in a circle of scorched earth that didn't look like the site of any normal fire.

Robin jabbed the blackened mud of the crater with his stick. "Look at the way the stones are cracked. It's like someone used a giant blowtorch on the ground."

Alfie poked around in the earth with his cousins, but all he found were stones and an old rusty buckle that must have been in the soil for years. Just as they were about to give up their search for clues, Robin found something a bit different from the other rocks. Alfie watched as he brushed away the dirt and rubbed it on his handkerchief to clear away the soot.

"What is it?" asked Madeleine, pulling at his arm. "Come on, let me see!"

Robin had frozen, staring at the thing he held in his hand.

"What did he find?" asked Alfie as he saw the color drain from Madeleine's face.

Madeleine lowered Robin's arm so that Alfie could see the small, blackened object he was holding. It was cracked and partly melted from the heat of the fire, but there was no mistaking what it was. As Alfie stared down into Robin's hand, Mrs. Emmett's cracked blue glass eye glared right back at him.

CHAPTER FIVE

Alfie's Marvelous Inheritance

A cheer went up from the crowd that had gathered at the bottom of Hopcraft Hill as Uncle Herb's truck trundled past them on the way up to the castle. All of the Blooms' worldly possessions were bundled into the back. Alfie felt like a celebrity as he waved to the crowd, even though a chill was still running through his veins from the other night.

The police had been at the farm until very late. Alfie and the twins had to answer lots of questions about why they were at Mrs. Emmett's farm and the exact spot in which they found the glass eye. Alfie had felt sick after their grisly discovery. For all her usual bravado, Madeleine had trembled as she spoke. Robin had sat like a ghostly statue as Mrs. Emmett's eye watched them from a plastic evidence bag on the kitchen table.

When the police finally finished with their questions,

Inspector Wainwright tucked the bag into his uniform pocket and headed outside for a chat with Uncle Herb. Aunt Grace had given Alfie and the twins hot chocolate with whipped cream and marshmallows and made them watch cartoons for a while, hoping that it might stop them from having nightmares. It didn't.

Alfie climbed down from the back of the truck as his dad and uncle started to unload it. He sat on one of the boxes, watching his aunt scurry down the hill to join the cluster of villagers talking excitedly among themselves. The group opened up, then closed around her.

"She's off to tell them all about Mrs. Emmett," said Madeleine, picking at the brown tape on one of the boxes. "She was on the phone to Gertie Entwhistle from the sweetshop all morning."

"What do you think happened to her?" asked Alfie, feeling an involuntary shiver as he gazed down across the fields toward the old lady's farm.

"I don't want to think about it."

"The inspector said it didn't seem like the rustlers," said Robin. "They haven't seen anything like it before. Maybe it was a freak lightning strike or something?"

"Look, can we just stop talking about it, please?" said Madeleine.

Alfie saw the look on Madeleine's face and quickly changed the subject by pulling out his folder of building plans.

"Here—why don't you pick out bedrooms? Then you can come and stay as often as you like."

The twins stared at him in amazement.

"Really? Are you serious?" asked Madeleine as Alfie handed her the plans. Robin looked as though he was about to explode as the three of them lay on the grass poring over the plans. There were certainly a lot of rooms.

"Look at how thick the walls are," said Robin. "They're wider than my whole bedroom. Alfie, when aliens invade Hexbridge, I'm moving in permanently!"

"Emily gave me these articles about the castle," said Alfie, pulling a news clipping out of the folder. "This one is my favorite. It says that three stonemasons came up here to steal bricks in 1890. Witnesses saw a flash of light just before the three of them ran down the hill screaming. One turned up in a farmer's field rolling in mud with the pigs, another was found wandering round the village pecking for corn kernels, and the third sat next to the lake for two days trying to catch flies with his tongue."

"No wonder it has never been broken into," said

Robin as they gazed up at the castle. "Not after stories like that."

The second the village clock chimed twelve, Alfie looked down the hill for any sign of Caspian Bone. Had he forgotten about their meeting?

"I see you have brought friends," said a voice from right behind him, making everyone jump. Alfie thought Caspian looked rather pleased by their reaction to his stealthy arrival.

"Well, Master Bloom," the lawyer announced as Alfie's dad and uncle hurried over. "All facilities have been updated and I can now present you with two sets of keys to your new home."

Each of the key rings held a large iron key, a silver disk bearing the Muninn and Bone coat of arms, and a rectangular piece of wood with two brass buttons. Alfie's also held a small silver whistle.

Alfie held up the wooden object. "What's this for?"

"Press the bottom button and find out," said the lawyer.

Alfie pressed it. There was a loud clanking noise. Small pieces of crumbled mortar and dust showered into the moat as he watched the drawbridge lower for the first time in centuries. It came to rest on the stone slab in front of him with a heavy *thud*, forming a very solid bridge across the moat. The portcullis that barred the castle gateway rattled upward to a round of applause from the crowd at the bottom of the hill.

"Whoa!" cried the twins in unison.

"As you can see, our contractors have aimed to make life in the castle as convenient as possible without destroying any of the original features," said Caspian.

Alfie raced across the drawbridge and through the arched entrance, closely followed by the twins and his dad. Reaching a huge courtyard, he stopped and gazed around in awe. Flowering plants climbed the walls and gently skirted the leaded windows. A massive oak tree stood at the center of the square. Sunlight streamed through its leaves, shedding dappled light onto the stone bench that partly encircled its trunk.

Beyond the paved area was a lush garden, alive with chirping birds, squirrels, and rabbits that bounced across the grass. Alfie nudged his dad and pointed out a gargoyle fountain set into a wall, spouting crystal clear water from its mouth into a rocky pool where large goldfish blew bubbles between the lily pads.

"It's beautiful, Alfie. The most amazing place I've ever seen."

"And it's ours, Dad!" Alfie thought he was going to burst with happiness.

"If you would care to try out your key, we can step inside," said Caspian.

Alfie approached the huge wooden double door at the far end of the courtyard. It unlocked with a satisfying *clunk*, and he swung it open to reveal a grand entrance hall with a large stone staircase that swept upward to a galleried landing. The sun streamed through three long stained-glass windows, painting the hall in a mosaic of rainbow-colored light.

"There are lots of staircases leading to different areas of the castle," said Caspian as Alfie stared up at the windows in awe. "For example, that small door in the corner opens onto a spiral staircase leading to the battlements. You will find that there are many different ways to get to some places and only one way to get to others. I believe you have the basic plans, but if you wish to see more detailed maps I suggest you try the castle library." Alfie noticed Robin's eyes light up at the mention of a library.

"These tapestries," said his dad thoughtfully, lifting the corner of the nearest one. "They're originals. They must be hundreds of years old, but they're in perfect condition."

"The castle has a . . ." Caspian paused. "I suppose you might call it a *protective environment.* You will find that everything here is remarkably well preserved."

"Yes, but how does—"

"If you'll excuse me, Mr. Bloom," interrupted Caspian, swatting the question out of the air with his hand. "I have other pressing matters to attend to. Several telephones have been installed." Caspian indicated a very old-fashioned dial phone on the wall. "If you require our help, just dial moon, star, and you will be put straight through to our offices."

Alfie had a quick look at the dial and noticed that after the zero there was a little silver moon, followed by a star and a sun.

"There aren't any wires or cables to the castle," said his dad. "So how do the telephones work?"

"Mr. Bloom," said Caspian, swishing his cape as he strolled back out of the door, "you really do ask the most mundane questions."

Madeleine and Robin were already running around shouting out each new discovery. Alfie was desperate to join them but had a burning question to ask Caspian. He followed the lawyer outside and saw that he was sitting on the bench under the oak tree, waiting.

"You wish to ask me if I was the raven outside of your school?" he asked. Alfie swallowed the question back down. "The answer is yes. I switched briefly out of raven form to see you with my human eyes. A rare lapse in judgment."

"You're a shape-shifter!" said Alfie, sitting down on the bench. He had seen the evidence with his own eyes but still hardly believed it. "Are there more people like you?"

Caspian flicked back his hair. "There is no one quite like me," he replied. "But if you wish to know if there are more shape-shifters in the world, then the answer is yes, many more. I'm sure you have heard of the African bouda, who take on the form of hyenas, or the Naga— the snake people of Nepal?"

Alfie felt a little embarrassed as he looked at Caspian blankly. The lawyer clicked his tongue.

"Do you learn anything practical at school? I suppose you are more familiar with tales of werewolves and vampire bats? Contrary to what those stories would have you believe, a shape-shifter's sole ambition is not to bite or maul as many humans as possible."

"So why were you watching me?" asked Alfie.

"We have been watching you for some time, Master

Bloom, to protect Orin Hopcraft's legacy." He stood up and brushed down his suit.

Alfie realized that Caspian soon tired of questions, so he was hardly surprised when the conversation suddenly concluded before he could say another word.

"Now, if you will excuse me, I am almost on time for an appointment. I prefer to be early." He gave the tiniest bow to Alfie. "I'm sure it won't be long before we meet again."

As Caspian reached the drawbridge, he stopped and called back. "The silver whistle on the key ring—to find out what it does, head up to the southern tower."

Alfie turned the little whistle over in his hand, then looked up to see a large raven sailing away over the hills.

By that afternoon, Alfie had explored the first floor, most of the second and third-floor rooms, and had fought his cousins on the battlements. His favorite room so far was the Great Hall with its gigantic table, huge chandelier, and intricately carved beams. A stone fireplace was set deep within an archway, two little benches with plush velvet cushions on either side. Robin informed him that it was an inglenook fireplace. Little stone gargoyles sat at either side of the mantel, pulling faces at them as they took turns looking up the chimney.

Alfie's cat, Galileo, had also been brought to the castle and seemed just as keen to investigate as Alfie and the twins. He trotted along beside them with his ears and tail perked up, darting in and out of every nook and cranny. After nearly tripping them up three times, he disappeared outside, where Alfie imagined he was carrying out an inventory of the mouse and bird population.

Alfie wasn't surprised that Robin's favorite room was the very impressive library. It was filled with bookcases that stretched right up to the high ceiling, with ladders that slid around rails to reach the highest books. Two large wooden griffins sat on either side of an archway between bookcases, proudly guarding some of the most beautiful books Alfie had ever seen. Their soft leather covers and parchment pages were incredibly well preserved. The ones he looked at were filled with elaborate calligraphy in many different languages, alongside paintings of everything from mythological creatures and places to everyday flowers and herbs. Orin must have traveled far and wide to build this collection, although Alfie noticed some slightly more recent books that suggested someone had continued to build the collection well into the seventeenth century before the castle was sealed.

Farther along the rows of shelves were collections of printed books. Alfie noticed Robin's jaw actually drop when he saw these.

"That's a Gutenberg Bible!" he cried out.

"A *what*?" asked Madeleine, bouncing on the couch.

"Only THE first book *ever* printed. There are less than fifty left in the world. Do you realize that this is over five hundred years old?"

Alfie laughed as Robin tried to look through the book without actually touching it with his fingers.

"I'm sure he's not really my brother," said Madeleine as Robin managed to open the cover with a large pair of tweezers he had found on the large oak table.

Alfie finally persuaded the twins to take a break from exploring to help unpack in his huge new bedroom. His clothes barely filled a quarter of the enormous wardrobe. As well as two balconies, his room had window seats, a large fireplace, and a secret panel that led to his very own huge, mosaic-patterned bathroom. The bedroom walls were covered in rich fabric rather than wallpaper. Alfie particularly liked the high, curved ceiling, which was painted with stars and planets, a bit like the one in

Caspian's office. They all jumped onto the massive four-poster bed and closed the curtains. Alfie looked around the enclosed space and realized the bed itself was bigger than his previous bedroom.

"So how come this Orin guy left you the castle?" asked Madeleine.

"I *still* don't know," said Alfie. "Dad does though, and if he doesn't tell me soon he can sleep in the cellars!"

Aunt Grace laid out sandwiches for dinner in the Great Hall. Granny made Alfie take the largest chair at the head of the table. As everyone tucked in hungrily, Alfie asked something he had been thinking about since that morning but had deliberately saved until his granny and auntie were present.

"Dad, could we have a castle-warming party for the whole village? Please?"

A look of horror spread over his dad's face as the twins cheered.

"It's a nice idea, Alfie," blustered his dad. "But that's a lot of people, and you know I'm no good at organizing parties. Remember your surprise tenth birthday?" Alfie remembered only too well. His dad had forgotten to send out the invites. Alfie hadn't actually minded at all. He had a feeling only Amy would have turned up anyway, and he wasn't sure what people would have made of his dad's peculiar sandwiches and science-based party games.

"Oh, go on, Will!" said Granny. "If you don't, everyone in the village will find an excuse to pop up here at some point. This way you can get it all over with in one go."

"Well, I suppose it'll be a good way for Alfie to make some new friends before starting school."

"Right then, we're agreed," announced Aunt Grace before he could back out. "Let's make it six o'clock on Saturday evening. We'll put up posters in the village."

Alfie beamed as his dad gave in.

"Oh, well," he said, perking up a little bit. "The documents Caspian Bone gave us mention that we'll have a butler to help out around here. Maybe he'll be good at organizing parties?"

A butler! thought Alfie in shock. What next? This was certainly a whole world away from their former life.

The twins had talked their way into staying over and insisted on setting up inflatable mattresses in Alfie's room so that they could all spend their first night in the castle together. After Uncle Herb's truck disappeared down the hill, Alfie's dad announced that he had a little surprise. He led them to a smaller room just off the Great Hall.

"Ta-da!" he beamed, swinging open the door. "I call it the Abernathy Room."

Alfie laughed in amazement at the familiar sight of all of their living-room furniture from Abernathy Terrace set out in exactly the same way as in the flat. The slightly worn modern furniture was dwarfed by the room and contrasted with the sumptuous fabrics on the walls, but Alfie thought it was brilliant. He flopped onto the soft sofa and smiled up at his dad.

"We're home."

CHAPTER SIX

The Six-Hundred-Year-Old Boy

The twins reluctantly went home early the next morning. Alfie had never seen his dad so excited as he helped him to set up a workshop in a lower room that looked out just above the moat. He seemed fascinated by everything in the castle. As much as Alfie had enjoyed spending time with his dad, he could tell that he was itching to get back to his own work, so he left him to it and spent the rest of the morning exploring on his own.

Alfie was still puzzled about who had modernized the castle. The alterations didn't look out of place, but they seemed to have been carried out by someone who didn't exactly understand their purpose. The light switches didn't operate lightbulbs, instead making the torches set in the walls burst into flame, even when removed from their brackets.

The big light switch in the Great Hall did something

very interesting. When Alfie flicked it upward, a hatch opened above the huge chandelier and a mechanical arm descended. With a click, a little flame appeared at its tip and the chandelier began to turn slowly so that the candles were lit one by one. When the switch was flicked the other way, the arm emerged with a snuffer to put out the candles. A small wheel on the wall lowered the chandelier so that the candles could be replaced.

When Alfie finally found the main bathroom, he was confronted with an enormous brass bath standing on clawed feet in the center of the room. A wooden archway towered above it, and this was covered in dials and wheels that altered the water pressure and made water shower down into the bath. His first shower was so cold that he leapt straight out with a yelp. "Argh, freezing!" The water stopped flowing as if someone had heard him. The pipes began to clank and, with a whooshing noise, steaming water rained down into the bath. Was the temperature setting voice-activated? "Too hot!" he shouted. The steam began to dissipate and the water cooled to a nice warm temperature. Alfie hopped back in. "Perfect. Er, thanks," he called out to the bathroom in general. The pipes seemed to make a little knocking noise in response.

Behind a tapestry at the end of the second-floor corridor was the door to the southern tower Caspian had mentioned. It opened with a loud and satisfying *creak*, revealing a stone staircase spiraling up into the darkness. Fighting his curiosity, he locked the door and pulled the tapestry back across it. It could wait until his cousins' next visit. He also saved the network of cellars until later. Dark, creepy places weren't as scary with other people, and he wanted to make the exploration of his new home last as long as possible.

Alfie wasn't sure how he knew, but he could swear that the castle seemed happy to have him there. He wondered if it was possible for a building to feel lonely.

A round room on the second floor felt strangely comforting. The walls were painted sky blue with intricate plants and flowers in soft colors. He stayed in that room for some time, reading comics on the window seat overlooking Lake Archelon.

"Alfie, where are you?" echoed his dad's distant voice.

"Up here!" Alfie kept on calling so that his dad could follow his voice. He doubted he'd ever get used to such a huge home.

"Funny I should find you here," said his dad as he appeared at the door with a tray of tea and slightly burnt fish-finger sandwiches.

"Why's that?" asked Alfie as he made room on the window seat and tucked hungrily into the late lunch.

"When you were little, we told you that you were born in Hexbridge when we were visiting your aunt and uncle. Well, that was only part of the story. You were born here, in this room, over six hundred years ago."

Alfie couldn't believe what he was hearing. "Wait, what? You're joking, right?"

"Far from it. Caspian confirmed something I'd long started to believe was a weird distorted memory."

"I don't understand—you're actually serious?"

"Utterly. Now it's time I told you about it, and it's a very strange story, so I'm afraid you'll have to be patient with your questions while I tell it."

Alfie nodded, still dumbstruck.

"Remember when we brought you here for your birthday a few years ago?"

"I remember," said Alfie. "There was a big Halloween party in the marketplace. Granny said it was a harvest festival."

"That's right, the Samhain harvest festival. It was taking place three weeks before you were due to be born and your mum didn't want to miss it. The hustle and bustle was a bit much, so we walked up here where it was quiet. She loved to see the castle in the moonlight. We sat next to the moat eating toffee apples and she told me one of your granny's stories about a prehistoric sea turtle that lived in Lake Archelon."

Alfie gazed down through the window into the dark waters of the lake and smiled. Granny Merryweather never let the truth get in the way of a good story.

"Halfway through, she stopped and grabbed my arm. You were on your way." He smiled down at Alfie. "You've always been impatient."

"I was about to run down and get the car when we realized the hill was surrounded by a thick mist. Everything had gone quiet—the music and voices from the village had stopped. I didn't know what to do. Then the castle drawbridge began to lower. There were lights and voices coming from inside. Before we knew it, a group of women had rushed out and were hustling us inside."

Alfie sat in stunned silence. He hadn't heard any of this before. The castle had opened for his parents on the day he was born? And the mist—was it something like his experience on the last day of the term? He stared up at his dad, hanging on every impossible word.

"Your mum was brought into this very room. I was amazed at how calm she seemed. I tried to follow, but the woman in charge made it very clear I was to wait outside. I spent two hours out there, waiting for news. That's when I really started to think about this place. The people I had seen were wearing clothes from hundreds of years ago. I started to wonder if they were ghosts!

"The next time one of the women ran past, I asked how long people had been living in the castle. She said that it had been lived in since it was built fifteen years ago. When I told her that the castle was hundreds of years old, she laughed and said, 'Well, of course *you* would say that, but here and now, it is fifteen years old.'

"So, what . . . you time traveled?" said Alfie. He half expected his dad to top it off by saying he had learned to fly too. "How? Was it something to do with the castle?"

"I don't know. I didn't ask, because that's when I heard you crying. The sound knocked every other thought clean out of my head. The ladies filed out of here and I came in to find your mum holding you all bundled up in a blanket. We couldn't believe how perfect you were for something so tiny. A few minutes later there was a knock on the door."

"Orin Hopcraft?" whispered Alfie. His dad nodded. "What did he look like?"

"He was wearing a tunic and had thick gray-brown

hair tied back with a strip of leather and a long, plaited beard. It was difficult to tell his age; he seemed old but there was something very youthful about him."

"Emily said that he was a druid. Was he really?" asked Alfie. He had read about druids at school: They were teachers, magicians, astrologers, warriors, and philosophers. He couldn't believe his dad might have actually met one.

"Perhaps the last, from what he told us. He said you were a child of two times, as much at home in his time as ours. But because your mother and I didn't belong there, the universe wouldn't let us stay much longer. Then he said that he had something to give you for safekeeping. His right hand glowed with a white light and he touched his fingertips to your forehead. The light seemed to be absorbed into you, and then everything around us started to fade.

"I woke up in a hospital chair. Jenny was sleeping in a bed nearby with you tucked up in a crib beside her. If it hadn't been for the blanket you had been wrapped in, we might have thought we had imagined it all. The only person we told was your granny—she's the only one who would have believed us. After your mum died, I hardly thought about it again. It was just a strange, hazy memory until a few days ago."

Alfie sat hugging his legs, chin resting on his knees. He had hardly moved during the tale and sat deep in thought trying to piece everything together.

"So, the thing he did with my head, did he tell you what it was?" asked Alfie.

"There wasn't time. We thought it was some sort of blessing."

The amazing story whirled around Alfie's head. *A child of two times . . .* He suddenly remembered their first meeting with Caspian. Hadn't the lawyer said something about him timeslipping on the last day of the term? Alfie decided it was time to tell his dad about the strange, misty place he had been transported to, but he strategically left out the fight with Vinnie and Weggis and the fact that he was nearly hit by a car.

"This is incredible," said his dad. "Caspian was right. You must have timeslipped, back to before the city existed and most of the land was forest!"

"You're seriously saying that you think I time traveled? How is that even possible?"

"Think about it. Although you grew up in our time, you were born in Orin's. Who knows? Perhaps this gave you some kind of natural ability to travel in time. The world is a magnificent, magical place with so much left to be discovered. The more you discover, the less you realize you know. Maybe Caspian can tell us more, although getting answers out of that man is like trying to squeeze water from a stone."

Alfie wondered what it meant to be a natural-born time traveler and if he'd ever be able to do it again. As he started on the last fish-finger sandwich, something more important hit him. "Hold on. If I'm really over six hundred years old, I'm even older than you!"

"You may have been born hundreds of years ago, but you're still eleven," laughed his dad. "So don't try pulling rank on me any time soon."

CHAPTER SEVEN

Murkle and Snitch

Following his dad's revelations, Alfie spent most of the afternoon with his eyes squeezed tightly shut as he tried to force himself back in time by sheer willpower. He finally gave up when all he managed to achieve was a headache.

At six o'clock that evening, Ashford the butler arrived in Hexbridge Castle's entrance hall. He was tall and slim with dark hair carefully smoothed back into a short ponytail and wore an elegant dark green suit with white gloves. Alfie thought it looked like something that someone who had only seen pictures of butlers in fairy-tale picture books might wear. His behavior was a little odd too.

"Alfie and William Bloom," he said (a little grumpily, Alfie thought). He shook Alfie and his dad's hands, looking them up and down and scanning their faces as though scrutinizing every inch of their appearance.

"How strange it is to meet you like this. For a man with absolutely no sense of humor, Caspian will have his little jokes." Alfie eased his hand back from Ashford's grasp and wondered what on earth he was talking about. "Well, here I am. So I suppose I had better start buttling. I take it I'm down here?" Alfie and his dad stared at each other in surprise as Ashford did something to the panel work under the stairs and opened a door that they hadn't even known was there. They watched as he swept downstairs with his suitcases.

After selecting a room and making himself at home on the lower floor, Ashford went straight to the kitchen and began to prepare a delicious-smelling dinner. Alfie's dad's request to have his meal brought to his workshop was firmly refused.

"Sir, I will not collect half-eaten plates of food from all over this castle. You will eat in the Great Hall at the same time as your son."

Ashford surprised Alfie with a conspiratorial wink. Alfie was very pleased with this rule. He hardly saw his dad when he was wrapped up in his inventions and was very afraid that he would soon fall into his old behavior, despite no longer needing to work several jobs. He smiled gratefully at the curious butler.

*   *   *

On Saturday, Ashford seemed to be making up for his initial slightly resentful attitude by conjuring fantastic dishes out of thin air. Wonderful smells drifted through the castle all day and set Alfie's stomach constantly rumbling. Alfie thought his aunt seemed a little put out when she turned up to find that she wasn't needed in the kitchen.

That evening, dozens of guests began to gather outside the castle long before the party was even due to start. When the clock in the Great Hall struck six o'clock, Alfie helped Ashford swing open the castle's heavy oak doors and lower the drawbridge. Aunt Grace's best friend, Gertie Entwhistle, was first across, carrying a huge cake dripping with chocolate. The crowd flooded over the drawbridge after her, murmuring with excitement.

"Welcome to Hexbridge Castle," announced Ashford with a small bow. "May I introduce your host, Master Alfie Bloom."

Everyone shook hands with Alfie and his dad as they streamed past, eager to see the inside of the castle for the first time.

Quite a few of the children at the party were pupils at Wyrmwald House, the school that Alfie was due to start in September with his cousins. They were all very excited to meet him and clamored for his attention, asking questions about the castle. Alfie felt uncomfortable at first—he wasn't used to being the center of attention. He had been known as the boy whose mum died at his last school and it had left him very lonely. He began to feel a lot better as he answered their questions. No one pitied or avoided him here. In Hexbridge he was known only as the boy who had inherited a castle.

He liked everyone Robin and Madeleine introduced him to very much—particularly the twins' neighbor, Jimmy Feeney, and Madeleine's best friend, Holly Okoye. He spent quite a while showing them around and even let them see one of the secret passages he had found. He wasn't sure if he was imagining it or not, but there was a sense of joy in the air, as though the castle was happy at having so much noise and laughter in its halls.

"Don't look now, Alfie," said Holly suddenly, "but Murkle and Snitch have caught your dad."

Alfie turned to see his dad standing between two very stern-looking women.

"Whoa, who are they?"

"You haven't heard?" exploded Jimmy. "Rob and Mads should have warned you by now. You don't want to go to Wyrmwald without knowing a thing or three about Murkle and Snitch!"

"We wanted to let him settle in first," said Robin. Alfie noticed him nudge Jimmy with his elbow.

"What's so bad about them?" he asked, eyeing the women nervously.

"They've been joint headmistresses at Wyrmwald House for years," replied Robin. "They even taught Mum and Dad. They're sisters and are supposed to be a bit strict, but Jimmy always exaggerates."

"Pah! You wait till September, then you'll see if I'm exaggerating or not! My brothers and sisters are always being put in detention for nothing."

"Nothing? Really?" laughed Robin.

Jimmy ignored him and continued. "Did you hear what they did to Charlie Belcher last year? My sister Sinéad saw it all, didn't you?" The tall dark-haired girl next to Alfie nodded.

"Sure did. Snitch thought she saw Charlie stealing someone's dessert, so they forced him to make himself sick and then made him run around the playing field for the whole afternoon."

"That can't be true," said Alfie.

"I didn't steal it," said a voice. The crowd of children parted to reveal the red-faced Charlie Belcher. "I swapped Ben Carter a trading card for it, but they wouldn't believe me."

"What did your parents do? You did tell them?"

"As soon as I got home. They went straight to the school to complain. When they came back, they were acting funny and grounded me for telling lies."

"Same thing happened when my ma went down there after they confiscated my brother Cormac's new red sneakers," said Jimmy. "She was fuming when she left, but she came back all weird and told Cormac off for losing them."

Alfie smiled politely at his new friend's exaggerations. Still, he decided that he would have to be very careful not to get on the wrong side of his new headmistresses.

"I'm not afraid of them," said a smartly suited boy in a haughty voice. "My father would have them sacked if they tried anything on me."

"Oh, shut it, Edward," said Jimmy. "You wouldn't dare mess with them. You cried your eyes out last week when Mrs. Sneesby confiscated your spud gun." Some of the others laughed loudly. Edward went bright red.

"I wasn't crying! I had hay fever." He stomped off before Jimmy could accuse him of lying. Alfie watched him join his equally haughty-looking parents. Edward's mother was prodding a sausage roll as though it was a large slug that had slithered onto her plate.

"That's Lord and Lady Snoddington," said Robin as Alfie noticed Edward's dad glaring around at the castle as though it had just insulted him. "They own Hexbridge Hall, the big manor house outside the village. Edward's always bragging about living in the biggest house for miles."

"Not anymore," snorted Madeleine. "Bet he hates you, Alfie!"

From the way Edward was scowling at him, Alfie was sure she was right.

"Alfie!" called his dad, beckoning frantically from across the room. "Come and meet your new headmistresses."

Alfie groaned and headed over.

"Good luck," whispered Holly.

"Alfie, this is Miss Evelyn Murkle and Miss Edwina Snitch." Alfie could understand why his dad seemed a bundle of nerves as he made the introductions. Although their appearance was very different, each of the women looked as mean and malicious as the other. Miss Murkle was short and round with red cheeks and wild frizzy hair. Miss Snitch was tall, pale, and wore her dark hair scraped back into a tight bun. Her nose was sharp, her fingernails were very sharp, but Alfie soon realized that the sharpest thing about her was her voice.

"A pleasure to meet you, young man." Her voice set his teeth on edge like nails scraping down a blackboard.

"A pleasure indeed," added Miss Murkle with a grimace that clearly stated it wasn't a pleasure at all. He shuffled back a little to try to put his dad between him and the two intimidating women.

"Your headmistresses have been asking all kinds of questions about the castle," said his dad. "Why don't you give them a guided tour? You can ask about your new school."

"That will be unnecessary," the sisters answered at exactly the same time. Alfie thought Miss Snitch looked thoroughly disgusted at the idea of spending time with him. "Now if you would excuse us." They turned and strode away, each in perfect time with the other. Alfie heard his dad give a huge sigh of relief.

"Ahem!" Alfie turned to see Lord and Lady Snoddington and a sulky Edward. Ashford was standing in front of them. Lord Snoddington prodded the butler in the back and snapped, "Go on, man, get on with it!"

Alfie thought he saw a sudden sharpness in Ashford's face. It passed as quickly as it had appeared and the butler adopted a charming smile. "Sirs," he announced, "Lord Tarquin and Lady Lucretia Snoddington would have me make their presence known to you."

Alfie gazed wistfully over at his friends and tried to remain polite as Lord and Lady Snoddington rambled on about their heritage and quizzed his dad on the Blooms' lack of it. They seemed determined to find out how they had inherited the castle. Alfie decided not to mention Orin Hopcraft and got around their questions by telling them that it used to belong to a distant relative.

Eventually, conversation turned to what Lord Snoddington referred to as gentlemanly pursuits.

"So, Alfred, have you ever been fox hunting? It's a fine sport. Young Edward has been riding alongside me since his eighth birthday. How would you like to come on the next hunt?"

Edward managed to look even sulkier.

"No, thank you, Lord Snoddington," said Alfie. "Isn't it illegal? Besides, I like foxes. Me and Mum used to leave food out for one that visited our garden."

"Why on earth would you encourage a fox into your garden?" Lady Snoddington's spindly eyebrows looked as though they were going to disappear into her hair. "They're vermin! Disease-ridden vermin!"

"I think you'll find that foxes are very intelligent creatures," said a woman with sparkling green eyes and vivid red hair. Alfie liked the way she wore it rolled back from her face like an old-fashioned film star.

"*Pffht!* I guessed you'd be of that ilk," exclaimed Lord Snoddington. He feigned a glance at an invisible watch and announced, "Goodness, is that the time? Thank you for inviting us into your humble home, young Alfred. Our chauffeur is waiting. Wouldn't do to leave the Bentley in view of all and sundry."

"Bloody tree huggers," Alfie heard him mutter as they left.

"I'd like to assure you that there are some relatively normal people in the village," said the red-haired woman with a grin. She held out her hand. "Hazel Reynard. I teach English and history at Wyrmwald House."

"It's a pleasure to meet you, Miss Reynard," said Alfie's dad. Alfie followed his dad's lead and shook the teacher's hand a little clumsily.

"Miss Murkle and Miss Snitch might not have

wanted the grand tour, but I'd love to see the library if Alfie doesn't mind showing me around instead?"

At that moment a slightly worse-for-wear Gertie Entwhistle dragged Alfie's dad away to judge whether her beet-and-chocolate cake or Mrs. Arbuckle's lemon meringue pie was nicer.

The twins joined them as Alfie led the way upstairs. Nearing the library, he was surprised to hear voices coming from inside. Miss Reynard put her finger to her lips and they crept toward the door to listen. It sounded as though furniture was being moved and drawers opened and closed.

"There must be something round here that can tell us where it is and how to open it," said an irritated voice.

"Of course there is—you're not looking hard enough," snapped someone else.

"Do you think there's a key?"

"That's why we're looking, to find out! Now stop wasting time and keep a lookout. Brats are swarming over this place like ants, and that Merryweather woman seems to be there every time I turn around."

Footsteps approached the door. Miss Reynard quickly flung it open and breezed into the room as though in midsentence. ". . . and *that* is the gruesome reason it is called a portcullis. Oh, hello, Miss Murkle. Sorry, did the door hit you? Miss Snitch, how lovely to see you at a social event. Have you met our host and his cousins? They'll be attending Wyrmwald in September."

Alfie was growing more and more impressed with Miss Reynard. Murkle rubbed her bruised nose and glared. Snitch's voice cut through the silence.

"Yes, we have met the boy. I'm afraid we got rather lost and noticed several children running amok in here. We sent them packing and are making sure they haven't damaged anything."

Miss Reynard smiled. "I'm sure Alfie is very grateful."

"Er, yes, thank you so much," said Alfie, taking his cue and earning a glare from Snitch that nearly knocked him over.

"Well, everything seems to be in order, so we'll be going." Miss Snitch cast one final sharp glance at Alfie as she left the room. Murkle waddled after her as Robin whispered in Miss Reynard's ear.

"Miss Murkle, I think you forgot something," she called, pointing at something the headmistress was trying to conceal under her cardigan.

"My mistake," spluttered Murkle. "It was on the floor when we came in. I, um, wasn't sure where to put it." She grudgingly handed over a roll of paper. Alfie watched them march away down the hallway and wondered what they had really been up to.

"What did you take from Miss Murkle?" he asked, when he was sure that they had gone.

"They appear to be plans of the castle." Miss Reynard rolled them out carefully onto the table. "I wonder what they were looking for."

"Whatever it was, it sounds as if they didn't find it," said Alfie.

"That's true, but it could be a reason to be careful around them. Murkle and Snitch are not the sort of people you want to take an interest in you."

Alfie was surprised to hear her refer to the headmistresses by their last names alone.

"Now that's enough about them." She smiled. "Let's see what treasures this room holds."

She browsed the books with great delight before admiring the library itself.

"Do you know the symbolism behind that?" she asked, pointing at an ornate painted carving above the fireplace. It was of three women around an old-fashioned spinning wheel. Alfie shook his head.

"Those are the Fates, three mythological sisters. The Greeks believed that they mapped out our lives at birth and decided how good or fortunate someone would be. Clotho, the youngest, is spinning the thread of life. She decides how happy a life will be. Her sister, Lachesis, is measuring it to decide how long the person will live. The oldest woman is Atropos. She cuts the thread when it is time to die."

Alfie stared, transfixed by the sisters as Miss Reynard spoke.

"The Greek philosopher Philostratus said that if the Fates decreed someone would win a race at the Olympic Games, then they would win even with a broken leg. If a man was destined to become a great archer, he would never miss his target even if he lost his eyesight."

Madeleine looked thoughtful. "So if I was destined to fail my exams, there's no way I could ever pass, no matter how hard I work?" she said with a smile. "It would be pointless trying, really."

"Hmm . . . well, as we can't talk to these ladies, there's no way of knowing if you are destined to fail math," said Miss Reynard, "so don't even think of not studying."

Alfie shot a last look at the Fates and gave an involuntary shiver as he headed back to the party. The thought of an entire lifetime mapped out and unchangeable was terrifying.

CHAPTER EIGHT

A Letter from the Past

Alfie's dad spent a lot of time in his workshop over the next few weeks. Alfie noticed how much happier he seemed being free to work on his devices every day, but couldn't help feeling a little sad they weren't spending as much time together as they had since the letter from Muninn and Bone. At least Ashford was enforcing the rule that he eat regular meals with Alfie in the Great Hall, and Dad was even starting to put on weight. Alfie had insisted that the butler eat his evening meal with them, and they clustered around one end of the huge table each evening. Ashford had warmed up considerably. But while he seemed incredibly interested in every aspect of their lives, he answered very little about himself.

"I'm far too boring a subject for dinner conversation," he announced when Alfie asked where he was from. "You'd fall asleep in your mashed potatoes. Now, tell me all about your last school. What were your favorite subjects?"

One day a little parcel covered in stamps arrived from Amy, who was still touring Asia with her gran. It contained a wooden beaded bracelet and a tiny vest. The letter informed him that the bracelet was from a temple in Beijing and the vest was a gift for Galileo from a cat café they had visited in Hong Kong. It cost him more than a few scratches to wrestle Galileo into the vest so that he could take a picture for Amy—the cat did not seem at all impressed with his gift. Amy had also enclosed some photos of their travels. His favorite was of her clambering over gigantic tree roots that sprawled over a temple she had visited in Thailand. At the bottom she had written, *I think this is what Gran meant when she said she wants me to discover my roots.* He laughed as he stuck the picture on his wardrobe door. He wished Amy wasn't away for the whole summer, as he was dying to talk to her about the castle and his dad's revelations.

After dreading a long boring summer alone in the city, Alfie found himself with barely a free minute in Hexbridge. He spent as much time at the farm as the castle, where Uncle Herb set him to work with the twins.

His days were filled with stacking hay bales, collecting eggs, and fixing fences.

One sunny afternoon in August, as Alfie and his cousins took a break from painting the cattle shed, a hunting horn blasted out from the forest. It was followed by dogs barking as they crashed through the undergrowth. Robin jumped to his feet. "It's the Snoddingtons and their friends. They're starting one of their hunts."

"Oh, the poor fox!" Madeleine shouted down from the tree she was sitting in. "I hope it bites old Snoddy on the backside and gives him rabies."

Alfie kept an eye out for the fox over the rest of the afternoon, hoping it would run onto the farm so they could hide it. Sadly it didn't. When the horn sounded again and the dogs started yelping, Alfie assumed that the fox had met a gruesome end. He finished painting in gloomy silence.

Dinnertime brought a wonderful surprise. The Merryweathers' neighbor Dermot Feeney and his son Jimmy came by with a tale to tell. In between fits of laughter, Dermot told how the fox had led the entire company straight through his fields just as he was spraying manure. Alfie couldn't control his glee as he heard about the moment the riders in their spotless red jackets and white britches found themselves sprayed with stinking manure. Everyone was in stitches as Jimmy impersonated Lord Snoddington spitting manure and calling to the others to retreat.

"Stop, stop!" shrieked Aunt Grace, tears streaming down her face. "My cheeks are hurting!"

When Alfie got back to the castle that evening, he could barely keep his eyes open. Although it was only half past seven, his dad insisted that he have a bath and go straight to bed. Galileo had already taken up his usual spot at the end of the bed by the time Alfie turned out the lights.

In the middle of the night, he was woken by a noise. *Tap-tap-tap.* He sat up in bed and listened . . . *Tap-tap-tap.* Galileo let out a low growl and slunk toward the window, his tail bushy. Alfie slipped out of bed and pulled the curtains aside. Galileo was already standing on the window seat, paws on the windowsill. Alfie gazed into the night. There was nothing there. Maybe it was the wind blowing ivy against the window?

Tap-tap-tap! Galileo hissed and Alfie nearly leapt out of his skin as he saw a large raven perched outside on the window ledge. It held an envelope in its beak and was staring up at him with eyes like shiny black beads.

"Caspian?" asked Alfie, opening the window and taking the envelope. Galileo leapt up and hung from the windowsill with one paw, frantically trying to swat the bird with the other.

"CRAAAUGH!" squawked the raven angrily, before flapping away into the night. Alfie broke the seal and pulled out a folded parchment and a Muninn and Bone compliments slip. The slip read:

Alfie,

I trust my messenger finds you well. Enclosed is the first of a number of communications left in our care by Orin Hopcraft. The rest will be delivered at times specified by the Great Druid. I trust they will help quell your insatiable curiosity.

Sincerely,
Caspian Bone

Alfie sat down on the window seat. A message from Orin himself, written hundreds of years ago! He carefully unfolded the parchment and blinked in surprise when he saw what was on the page. Nothing. Could the ink have completely faded away after all those years? He turned the page over, but the other side was blank too. Maybe there was a secret message on it, like the ones he used to write in lemon juice with Amy. He flicked the light switch and the torches on the walls burst into flame. Holding the letter close to the flames, he waited for brown letters to be scorched across the page. Again, nothing.

Disappointed, Alfie folded the parchment and got back into bed. Maybe his dad could figure it out in the morning. Galileo remained on the window seat guarding against more avian visitors. As Alfie began to doze off, Emily Fortune's words suddenly drifted into his mind. What was it she had said about the talisman—it was a key and a lens that could reveal secrets and focus energy? He sat bolt upright, grabbed the paper, and whipped the talisman out of his pajama top. Holding it up to his eye, he looked at the parchment through the lens. He almost dropped it when he saw what was there. Tinted purple by the lens, the parchment was now covered in glowing calligraphic writing. Heart pounding, Alfie clenched the talisman like a monocle between his cheek and eyebrow and began to read:

Dear Alfie,

How good it is to break through the barrier of time and speak to you at last. I requested that this letter be delivered to you shortly after the transference of your inheritance. How do you like our castle? I am afraid I placed rather a burden upon you during your first visit. The castle is reparation for my presumption, which I hope to explain to you in this letter.

There has always been magic in the universe. It existed before our world was created and will be there at the end of time. The druids, as we now call ourselves, were among the guardians of some of the ancient magics—magics so powerful they should never be used. These have passed from master to apprentice for thousands of years. Just before my mentor died, he passed the magic he had guarded on to me. A creation magic—it feeds upon energy, whether heat, lightning, other magic, or even life itself. Once fed, it can use this energy to create whatever you wish. Or to destroy. Such magic, as I am sure you can understand, must remain hidden. It would be truly terrible in the wrong hands.

As I continued to develop my own skills in potion making and elemental magic, a dangerous druid came to see me: Agrodonn. I didn't know it at the time, but he had begun hunting down other druids and taking the lesser great magics that they guarded. First, he hoped to bargain with me and share my magic, talking of all that we could create with it. When I refused, he tried to take it by force. But I was too powerful for him. Most of his magic had been stolen. Magic that is not earned is dangerous and hard to control. I drove him out.

On his next visit he brought powerful allies that he had bent to his will. Again he demanded I hand over the magic. I refused, and his allies torched the villagers' crops and slaughtered their livestock. When he told me that the people would be next, I felt rage. The magic unfurled inside me, asking to be used. As Agrodonn laughed at the carnage below us, it took over my body and blasted into him, *stripping away and feeding on every last bit of magic inside him. He fled, as did his allies when they came out from under his spell.*

Agrodonn did not return. The magic I guarded had been well fed, so I had no choice but to use it. With the power it had drained from him I created this castle. It has become the villagers' home in times of trouble and a place of learning. However, the Fates soon decreed that the magic should disappear from the world for a while and pointed to a living hiding place. A child. One who would have the courage and strength to become the new guardian without using the magic for his own ends. Magic has never been passed on to one so young, without any training, but the Fates were clear. You were to be the new guardian.

Alfie's head was spinning as he tried to swallow down the panicky feeling rising inside him. So the light Orin had passed into him was the magic. That's why Orin had left him the castle, because he had made him into a hiding place for something a terrible druid had killed for! Alfie knew now why Orin hadn't explained it to his mum and dad: They would never have allowed him to pass the magic on to their newborn son.

> *On Samhain, the borders between worlds are already thin and time becomes more fluid. I was able to tear a rift in time to where your mother and father were waiting. As the three of you slipped back into your own time, the magic disappeared from the world for six hundred years. No one in your time knows it exists. You may notice its presence more as you near your thirteenth birthday, but the talisman helps to control and conceal it, so you are safe. Although you could not give your permission (and I beg your forgiveness for that), I hope that you can accept your role as one of the last guardians of the ancient magics.*
>
> *I have much more to say, but for now I leave you to absorb what I have written here. I hope that you will find my study soon. The knowledge it contains is perhaps my greatest gift to you.*
>
> *Your friend, always,*
> *Orin Hopcraft*

Alfie took a deep breath and read the letter another two times. He had never felt any magic inside him, and he doubted anyone would believe it even if he told them, but the thought of harboring something so dangerous scared him. *A magic that could create or destroy anything but first needed to feed on energy, even life itself.* No wonder Orin wanted to hide it so badly. If Orin had used it to build the castle, what could it create if it fed on electricity, or even power stations? Powerful weapons? Invincible armies? What would people do for that kind of power? He shivered despite the warmth of his bed. The druid had said that he was safe. Alfie hoped he was right.

CHAPTER NINE

Skirmish in the Skies

"It looks ancient," said Robin, lying on the floor and peering into the open mouth of a dusty bearskin rug.

It was several days after the letter from Orin Hopcraft. Alfie hadn't told his dad about the letter. What if he panicked and wanted Caspian to take back the castle along with the magic? Alfie couldn't bear the thought of losing the castle and the closeness he was starting to feel with his dad. Besides, Alfie was enjoying having his own secret for once. Orin had said that no one knew about magic in his time, so he had decided that he could deal with being treated as a hiding place if a castle was the reward. Although he still wasn't sure what it meant to be guardian of an ancient magic.

Robin and Madeleine were staying over again and they were all on a midnight mission to explore the castle. Alfie had been unable to find Orin's study, so he had decided they would explore the southern tower. The second he unlocked the hidden door, Madeleine shot past him and up the stairs like a rocket.

The spiral staircase seemed to go on forever as they investigated the dark, mostly empty rooms on the way up. Alfie had brought the silver whistle, as instructed by Caspian. He blew it in each room they passed but nothing happened—it didn't even make a noise. Maybe it was broken? The last room at the top of the tower was different from the others, cozily furnished and decorated with artifacts from many different countries: painted shields, colorful masks, silk paintings from China. A harpsichord stood in the far corner, along with a funny-looking set of bagpipes. In front of the fireplace was the bearskin rug that Robin was currently staring into the mouth of.

"He must have been very frightening when he was alive," said Madeleine, patting the rug as Alfie gave one last blast on the whistle.

"Very kind of you to say so, lass," said a deep rumbling voice as the bear's head lifted and turned around to face them.

Alfie nearly choked on the whistle as Robin scrambled backward, knocking over Madeleine in his haste to get away from the talking rug. Alfie watched the bear in astonishment as he floated gently into the air, gave a loud yawn, and began to shake himself like a dog that had just had a bath. Centuries of dust and loose hair swirled around the room.

When he finally seemed satisfied, the bear turned to Alfie, whose own hair was now full of dust.

"Well then, young lad. I have been asleep too long and could do with getting the wind through my fur. Since you woke me, you can decide where we're going."

Alfie stared at the bear's shiny glass eyes and grinning mouth, wondering whether to answer or run for his life. The bear seemed to be enjoying the reaction he was getting and rolled his eyes before speaking very slowly and loudly, as if to someone hard of hearing. "WHERE WOULD YOU LIKE TO GO?"

"You mean you can take us anywhere?" asked Robin, finding his voice.

"Now you're getting it," growled the bear with a grin. "Within reason, of course. The moon could take a while so you'd need plenty of sandwiches, and a sweater—it's cold up there."

Alfie gathered his wits. The bear couldn't exactly eat him—it didn't even have a stomach. He decided to test it. He opened a window and pointed down to the Merryweather farm.

"Can you take us over there, to the tree house on that farm?"

The bear looked unimpressed and made a loud yawning noise.

"How about Newcastle?" suggested Robin. "It's about half an hour east of here."

For a creature without shoulders, Alfie thought the bear gave a very good shrug. "Pah!"

"Okay," said Robin, "how about to—"

"LONDON!" shouted Madeleine, jumping into the air.

"Don't be stupid, Maddie. That would take hours."

"Not as the bear flies," it laughed. "Good to see there's someone with an adventurous spirit among you. Now, all aboooooard!"

He began to rise slowly into the air. Alfie finally decided that the bear couldn't be that dangerous if Orin had kept him in the castle. He took a deep breath and hopped on, closely followed by the twins.

"You'd better hold tight—I haven't done this in a while!"

Alfie clutched the bear's fur as he hovered three feet off the ground and rotated to face the window. A warm wind seemed to build up around them as the rug rippled in the air.

"Everybody ready? Everybody steady?" asked the bear. Madeleine launched herself forward, wrapping her arms tightly around the bear's neck as he roared, "Here . . . we . . . GO!"

With that, they shot out the window, swooping over the rooftops of the castle and into the night sky. Alfie laughed with excitement and fear, his stomach turning somersaults as the ground dropped away beneath them. The twins whooped and screamed beside him as they all gripped on tightly. Alfie felt as though they were on the strangest roller coaster in the world. With a roar, the bear picked up speed, circling the castle one last time before heading east toward the coast.

"I thought we'd take in a sea breeze on the way down. I'd like to blast away some of my cobwebs."

Within minutes the patchwork of fields beneath them disappeared and the bear turned south over the North Sea. They lay on their stomachs, peering through the thin clouds that whizzed by beneath. Alfie could just make out the distant lights of ships sailing far below them.

"We're going very fast," said Robin. "Why aren't we getting blown about by the wind?"

"Magic!" replied the bear, turning its head. "Reach out your hand and you'll see what I mean."

They stretched their arms out over the edge of the rug. Alfie felt the wind rushing past his fingers—the farther he reached, the stronger and faster the wind seemed to be. He tucked his hand into his armpit to warm it back up. It was like being inside their own warm little bubble.

Every now and then, plane lights blinked in the distance. As they drew close to one, Alfie could make out all the little windows along the sides. Some were lit up and he could see passengers dozing or reading inside. *What a boring way to travel*, he thought with a grin.

"Lady and gentlemen, we are beginning our descent into the city of London," announced the bear.

"Already?" said Madeleine.

Alfie leaned over the side of the rug to see the city lights twinkling up at him. His heart leapt into his mouth as they swooped over the huge dome of St. Paul's Cathedral and down to skim the River Thames.

"Ooh, this is all new," said the bear as they flew under Tower Bridge, then looped back over the top before slowing to follow the curve of the river.

"You've been here before?" asked Alfie.

"Not since the fire. They didn't do too bad a job on

the rebuild. Although *that* seems to have moved a bit."
He pointed a claw toward the modern reconstruction of
Shakespeare's Globe.

"You mean the Great Fire?" asked Robin. "That was
in 1666! How old are you?"

"There's Big Ben!" Alfie interrupted as the brightly lit
Palace of Westminster and its famous clock tower loomed
up on their right. "Can you take us to the top?"

"The very top?" asked the bear, gliding up toward the
spiky spire that topped the tower.

"Nooo!" they all called at once.

"How about there?" Madeleine pointed to the balcony that ran around the edge of the uppermost roof.
"Holly came here with her mum last year on a special
tour. She had her picture taken inside the clock bit. Wait
till I tell her I went up even higher!"

"As if she'd believe you," said Robin as the bear
landed gently on the balcony.

Alfie felt as though he was still moving as he stepped
shakily off the rug and looked down through the railings
toward the ground. "Wow, I didn't realize it was this high."

"It's nearly a hundred yards tall and over one hundred and fifty years old," said Madeleine with authority.
"Holly told me. She knows loads about Big Ben now."

Robin snorted. "Really? She doesn't even know that it's not called Big Ben. That's the name of the bell, not the tower."

Alfie tuned out the twins squabbling as he enjoyed the view. Although it was a warm evening, there was a light mist in the air. He enjoyed its cooling embrace as he leaned against the railings and gazed across the Thames.

"That's the London Eye," said Madeleine, popping her head over his shoulder. "Holly went on that too."

"Who cares?" shouted an exasperated Robin.

Alfie slipped away as the twins began arguing about the direction in which Buckingham Palace lay. Wandering back to the spot where they had left the bearskin rug, he was met with a bizarre sight. It appeared that the bear had decided to dust himself off completely and was flying around the tower, twisting, turning, and looping the loop. Little clouds of dust and hair were left behind as he flipped from one spot to another. Alfie spotted a pedestrian far below who had stopped walking and was trying to make out the strange shape flapping around far above him. Alfie laughed as he imagined tomorrow's headlines: BIG BEN'S BRUSH WITH GIANT BAT. The bear finished shaking himself down and began to chase the moths flitting around the illuminated clock face. Alfie gave a loud whistle.

"Hey! Do you want everyone in the city to see you?"

The bear grinned and floated over to him.

"How do I look?" he asked proudly as Madeleine skipped toward them.

"Very handsome," she laughed. "Next time I'll bring a comb to brush your fur."

"Maybe you should try using one yourself," quipped Robin to a black look from Madeleine.

The takeoff was gentler this time as the bear floated vertically into the air. Soon they were level with the spire at the very top of the tower. Alfie reached out and touched one of the six golden flowers around the orb at the top, wondering if anyone else had seen them this close in the last one hundred and fifty years. He pulled a silly face as Robin held his camera at arm's length and snapped a picture of the group.

"So how come you're a rug?" asked Madeleine, lying on her stomach and scratching behind the bear's ears as they sailed home through the clouds. "Did someone kill you?"

"Maddie!" hissed Robin. "You're being rude!"

"Not at all," chuckled the bear. "I can't remember much about it. Orin told me I had been killed by a hunter who turned my skin into this rug."

"That's horrible," said Madeleine as she stroked his head.

"So how come you can fly and talk?" asked Alfie, thinking how wonderful it was to know a flying carpet that he could actually hold a conversation with.

"Orin used his magic on me. He could tell that my spirit was still in my body and wanted to help me speak and travel. I don't know how I understand humans though. Maybe all bears do but can't talk back? I was his friend for many years and went with him on his travels. When he left, he told me to sleep and wait for you."

"So Orin didn't die here?" said Alfie, surprised to hear that the druid had left the castle empty.

"Oh, no, he didn't die here." The bear gave an amused smile but didn't say anything else.

"Do you have a name?" asked Alfie, suddenly embarrassed that he hadn't thought to ask sooner.

"Orin named me Artan. It means little bear."

"Artan . . . A lovely name for a lovely bear," said Madeleine sleepily as she rested on top of his fuzzy head.

"Ah, that cheers me up, lass. I've been feeling a bit flat lately." They all groaned, the rug rippling beneath them as Artan chuckled at his own joke.

"Now approaching Hexbridge," he called after a few minutes.

The words were barely out of his mouth when a large shape shot out of the mist in front of them. It flew over the tops of their heads, creating a gust of wind that sent Artan whirling.

"Hold on!" shouted the bear as he fought to regain control.

"What was that?" yelled Alfie, straining to make out the shape in the mist. It had turned around and was headed straight back in their direction at some speed.

"Whatever it is, it's trying to knock us out of the sky!" called Artan. "It's coming at us again. Hold on tight, I'm going to try some special maneuvers!"

Alfie and Robin flung themselves forward and gripped the rug on either side of Madeleine as the huge dark shape hurtled toward them. Just before it hit, Artan whipped himself aside like a bullfighter's cloak. Alfie barely held on as they dangled in midair for a split second before flopping back onto the rug as it righted itself.

"Everyone still on board?"

"Just about," shouted Alfie, wriggling away from the edge.

"It's coming about again. I'll try to lose it in the clouds."

Alfie dug his fingers into the bear's thick fur and

squeezed tightly, and Madeleine and Robin did the same as the bear started his sharp climb into the mist. The dark shape seemed to be picking up speed again as it followed their ascent.

"Can you go faster, Artan?" called Robin. "It's catching up!"

"I'm going as fast as I can with three passengers," the bear bellowed back. "Let it get as close as you dare— then shout out a second before it hits."

Alfie looked back to see the shape rapidly gaining on them and caught the smell of rotten eggs on the air. It seemed to be getting stronger as the shape drew closer. Suddenly a huge pair of yellow eyes glared at him through the mist. There was a screech as another pair appeared to the right.

"There are two of them!" he shouted up through the roaring wind. "They're really close!" with a sudden lurch the creatures were almost upon them. "Now, now, NOW!" screamed Alfie. Artan immediately stopped climbing and dove toward the ground. There was a loud screech as the creatures whipped past, disappearing into the clouds. Madeleine punched the air in triumph.

"Maddie!" screamed Robin. The quick turn followed by the downdraft of the creatures' wings sent the rug into a spin and Madeleine lost her grip. The bear pulled up out of his descent as Alfie grabbed for his cousin's arm, but Madeleine was sliding away from him. She clutched at Artan's fur and finally caught on to Alfie's shoe as she hung off the edge of the rug. Alfie reached down and grasped for her hand a second too late. The shoe slid from his foot. With a terrified yell, Madeleine dropped like a stone through the mist.

"Hold tight!" shouted Artan. Alfie clung on with hands and knees as they nosedived toward Madeleine. He could hear the creatures' frustrated screeches way above as they searched for their lost prey.

"We're not going to catch her in time!" shouted Robin as they cleared the clouds. The treetops loomed below as Madeleine tumbled toward them. She was falling too quickly. Alfie pressed his body against the rug, trying to streamline himself as much as possible as he willed the bear to move faster. Robin followed his lead.

Artan shot through the air with a speed Alfie hadn't thought possible. He risked another look down and could hardly believe it—they were closing in on Madeleine. Her screams grew louder as they whistled through the air.

"Come on, come on!" he whispered under his breath,

hardly daring to hope. In seconds that passed like hours, Artan was finally below Madeleine. Alfie and Robin rolled to the sides as her flailing body thumped down onto the rug between them, bouncing them into the air so that they almost fell off. As Artan skimmed the tree-tops and shot back into the sky, Robin threw his arms around Madeleine and hugged her as hard as he could.

"Careful there, lad," called Artan. "You'll squeeze out whatever breath she has left." Robin loosened his grip and Madeleine started to make a noise somewhere between coughing and hiccuping.

"Thank you, Artan," said Robin in a quiet, serious voice, patting the bear's back. Alfie could see that he was as pale as Madeleine as they floated gently down toward the battlements of Hexbridge Castle.

"You're amazing, Artan." Madeleine threw her arms around the bear's neck as they landed. "Thank you."

"Think nothing of it, little one," said the bear, looking a little embarrassed but proud at the praise being heaped upon him. The twins both looked a bit wobbly as they hopped off Artan's back, but Alfie was relieved to see that Madeleine was starting to get some color back into her cheeks.

Alfie suddenly found the wind knocked out of him as

Artan wrapped himself tightly around them and gave a squeeze.

"It's good to see you again, old friends," he said in a serious voice before treating them to his biggest grin. "If you ever need me, just blow Orin's whistle and I'll come to you. We always have the greatest adventures!"

"But we've only just met," said Alfie in surprise as Artan began to float back up to his tower.

"True, but also false!" Artan called down as he performed a little flip and disappeared through the window to his room.

Alfie puzzled over Artan's strange words as they flopped onto their beds, the twins still using their inflatable mattresses in his room. None of them were ready for sleep after their terrifying experience.

Alfie decided that it was finally time to tell his cousins everything that had happened recently—his timeslip on the last day of the term, Caspian Bone's true form, and Orin's letter. The twins listened in wide-eyed silence, wrapped snug in their duvets as Alfie read the letter through the talisman's lens.

"I'm not sure I'd have believed it all yesterday," Madeleine breathed at last. "But after tonight . . ."

"So this is all true?" asked Robin. "You were really born here hundreds of years ago?"

Alfie nodded. "Dad told me that bit himself."

"And the magic Orin hid inside you—you can create *anything* with it?"

"Maybe. But after reading that letter, there's no way I'm going to try. It sounds as though he is going to send me more letters. Maybe he'll tell me more about it."

"Those creatures," said Madeleine. "What do you think they were?"

"I have no idea," said Alfie. "Did either of you get a good look at them?" The twins shook their heads.

"They could have been white-tailed eagles," said Robin. "They've got a wingspan of up to eight feet and there are quite a few up in Scotland. Maybe we got too near wherever they're nesting?"

Alfie began to tune out as Robin continued to explain away the strange creatures. Madeleine seemed happy to accept Robin's theory, but the twins hadn't seen the eyes of the things that had chased them. Alfie shivered despite his warm duvet. If they weren't birds, what were they?

CHAPTER TEN

WYRMWALD HOUSE

Since their flight, Alfie had continued searching high and low for Orin's study, hoping it might contain information on the creatures that had attacked them as well as the magic inside him. Robin and Madeleine had helped him scour the castle, and Ashford seemed rather perplexed by the number of times he came across them investigating every inch of the walls in various rooms. The search was finally suspended as shopping expeditions for new school uniforms overshadowed even talk of flying beasts, bearskin rugs, and a secret study.

Alfie was delighted when his dad bought him a brand-new uniform. He was used to ill-fitting second-hand clothes that had made him feel embarrassed and uncomfortable at his old school. Now he was given a new jacket, shoes, sports bag, and expensive-looking sneakers. The monthly allowance from Muninn and Bone must be good. His dad had even taken him to several hardware stores to buy all kinds of equipment for whatever he was building in his new workshop.

The morning of the first day of the term finally came around, and Alfie was enjoying kicking a ball around the playground with Robin and Jimmy. Madeleine and Holly were under the trees at the edge of the playground searching for early horse chestnuts among the spiky green casings. Alfie was already impressed with Wyrmwald House. It was an old redbrick building that seemed huge in comparison to his last school: a flat-roofed building with ugly pebble-dashed walls.

"Why don't we play over there away from the fence?" he suggested, as the ball sailed over it for the third time.

"Would you listen to him!" announced Jimmy as he squeezed through the railings and threw it back over. "That's Murkle and Snitch's office. If we played in front of it they'd use it as reason to give us detention—or worse."

"He's right," added Robin. "Last year Billy Reynolds accidently hit their window with a soccer ball. They made him cut the ball into exactly a thousand pieces with a pair of blunt scissors. Then he had to thread the pieces onto a bit of string and wear them around his neck for the entire term. It's hanging in the Hall of Penitence now."

"The Hall of *what*?" asked Alfie. He didn't like the sound of it one bit.

"Penitence. The whole corridor leading to the heads' office is like a gallery showing off the weird punishments they give out. They frame their favorites for everyone to see."

"No way!" Alfie still didn't quite believe the stories he had been told at the party. "The school inspectors would have them fired or shut the place down if they did that."

"I told you what happens when our parents complain, didn't I?" said Jimmy. "The school inspectors just get taken straight to their office and then leave without bothering to look around. My brother Cormac thinks they're bribing them, but I reckon they're hypnotists or something."

"I asked my mum if they were doing it when she was here with Auntie Jenny," said Robin. "She couldn't remember. Maybe they were nicer then."

"Mum?" said Alfie in surprise, all other thoughts dropping away as Robin mentioned her name. He had forgotten that she had been a pupil at Wyrmwald House nearly twenty-five years earlier. He felt a pleasant warmth at the thought of studying at the same school. He wondered if she had gotten into trouble with Murkle and Snitch very often.

A shrill whistle pierced the air, instantly silencing the playground.

"Keep still!" hissed Jimmy as Alfie looked around to see the older children frozen like statues. Miss Snitch was standing nearby with a whistle to her lips, her eyes narrowed as she scrutinized the playground. Miss Murkle began to weave slowly between the frozen children. "Here she comes," Jimmy muttered. "Don't move a muscle until you hear the second whistle."

Alfie stood perfectly still as Murkle moved closer, scanning the playground for movement. The girl nearest to him had been playing hopscotch when the whistle blew and hadn't been quick enough to put both feet on the ground. Sweat started to glisten on her forehead as she balanced on one leg. Murkle stopped in front of her, cocked her head to one side, and waited. Alfie winced in sympathy as he saw the girl's leg starting to wobble. The struggle to stay balanced under Murkle's unblinking stare was too much. Her leg finally gave way and she fell forward into her friend.

"DEEEEEEE-ten-SHUN!" yelled Murkle, pointing a stubby finger victoriously at the girls before searching for another victim. After what seemed like an age, there was another sharp blast of the whistle. The whole playground finally relaxed, and Alfie joined the stream of children flowing toward the main entrance to form straight lines facing the school.

"First years here, please!" called a familiar voice through the commotion. Alfie saw Miss Reynard standing in front of one of the lines and fought his way through the crowd to join it. "Stand as straight and smart as possible," she told the children. "The headmistresses will inspect you in a minute. Don't let them see anything out of place."

She gave Alfie, Robin, and Madeleine a smile and motioned to Jimmy to tuck his soccer ball into his bag. Alfie copied the other children, standing as neatly and quietly as possible, not daring to make eye contact with Murkle and Snitch as they approached.

"Hmm, a ragtag bunch of strays and scoundrels by the looks of them," said Murkle as she wandered down the line of trembling first years, her plump face screwed up as if she were sucking a lemon.

"Agreed," replied Snitch, keeping step with her sister on the other side of the line. She whisked a cap from a student's head and sent it whirling through the air, startling a family of sparrows as it caught in the branches of their tree. Holly Okoye was next. Alfie cringed as Snitch snatched an orange slide from her hair and used it to clean her ear as she continued down the line. "I believe some reeducation on the correct dress code will be necessary during afternoon assembly today, Miss Murkle."

After another achingly long minute of silence, during which Alfie hardly dared breathe, Snitch raised the whistle to her thin lips and gave it a sharp blast. With one last glare, she turned and marched up the school steps and through the large wooden doors followed closely by Murkle. Both teachers and pupils breathed a sigh of relief as they disappeared.

The homeroom teachers took their places at the head of each line. One by one, they led the way to class, starting with the oldest students.

"I didn't think we'd have to do this in secondary school," whispered Alfie as he watched the other lines marching through the doors.

"It's not every day," whispered Jimmy as Miss Reynard led the first years into their new school. "My brother said that they do it now and then, whenever they fancy picking on us."

Alfie found the school daunting, with its high

ceilings and wood-paneled walls. The smell of wax, disinfectant, and polish filled the cool corridors and seemed to be coming from everything from the tiled floors to the cast-iron radiators.

"The Doors of Doom!" said Jimmy dramatically as they passed the large double doors that led to the head-mistresses' office and the ominous Hall of Penitence.

Miss Reynard's classroom was right at the back of the school looking out onto the hills. It was bright and airy with an array of interesting objects on the many shelves: fossils, replica swords, tribal headdresses, an old gas mask, and model trains from Stephenson's *Rocket* to a Japanese bullet train. As Miss Reynard told them a little about her favorite objects, Alfie thought that she seemed to be just as excited by history as his dad was by the way things worked. He was very glad that she would be their homeroom teacher for the year.

The morning induction passed quickly as they moved on to copying down their weekly timetables and reading through the school handbook. Miss Reynard had come up with a name game for the whole class to play while getting to know one another. Alfie enjoyed hearing from all of his new classmates, with the exception of Edward Snoddington and his mean-faced friend Hugo Pugsley, who, Jimmy pointed out, had an expression rather like a pug dog chewing a wasp.

School lunch was a grim experience. Alfie had liked the lunch ladies at his last school, but the ones at Wyrmwald House were the surliest he had ever seen. His lunch consisted of a tough slab of boiled liver and a pile of carrots and sprouts that turned to mush as soon as he prodded them with his fork. Dessert was something wobbly and pink that tasted like antiseptic.

"Sorry, we forgot to warn you," said Madeleine as she ate her packed lunch. Aunt Grace must have remembered the school lunches only too well and had prepared sandwiches for the twins along with a large slab of fruitcake. They donated a slice to Alfie and he ate it gratefully, savoring the juicy raisins as he decided to ask Ashford if he would mind making packed lunches. He never wanted school lunch again.

As it was the first day of the term, an afternoon assembly had been called. The whole school filed into the hall and took their seats on rows of benches, each worn smooth by many years of fidgety bottoms. Alfie felt a little nervous when he realized the first years were in the front row right under the watchful eyes of the headmistresses. It didn't help that Edward Snoddington had chosen to sit next to him, apparently for no other reason than to look down his nose at him.

"Welcome back," growled Miss Murkle from the school stage. "We hope that your brains haven't rotted completely through lack of use. Just to make sure, we have arranged tests in every subject over the next week."

A few groans were heard but were instantly silenced as Miss Snitch stood up to take over from her sister.

"Any student scoring a C or below in any subject will spend two weeks in after-school detention brushing up on their studies."

"That's me missing soccer practice for two weeks," Alfie heard someone mumble behind him.

Alfie flinched involuntarily as Snitch turned her unblinking gaze onto the front row. "Due to the disregard of the school dress code they exhibited today, first years will also have a test tomorrow morning. I suggest you all memorize the contents of the school handbook."

Alfie groaned inwardly as the two headmistresses made everyone stand and recite the school rules after them. He had been planning on visiting Artan that evening and wasn't looking forward to having to study instead.

"You may sit," said Snitch, finally reaching the end of

the huge list of rules. Alfie sank gratefully onto the bench, then leapt up with a yell, rubbing the seat of his trousers. He turned to see a spiky horse chestnut casing on his chair and looked sharply at Edward, who was staring straight ahead, a sly smirk playing around the edges of his mouth.

"You, boy!" Miss Snitch screamed at Alfie with the accuracy of a sniper. "What are you doing with your backside?" Some of the first years began to laugh. Edward and Hugo laughed particularly hard. Only a couple of nervous coughs were heard from the pupils who had been at the school long enough to know better. They needn't have worried: Today Snitch was saving all her venom for Alfie.

"So, the king of the castle is also a jester, is he?"

"No, miss," said Alfie, his cheeks burning white hot with embarrassment. "There was a chestnut case on my—"

"Silence, funny boy! Your mother thought she was funny too, with all her little jokes. She stopped laughing after a year of detention!"

The whole hall gasped. A *year* of detention with Murkle and Snitch? Alfie couldn't believe that his mum had gotten into trouble at the school and was furious at the thought of the headmistresses picking on her. He hated Murkle and Snitch.

"Are you a bad seed like your mother?"

Alfie glared back at her.

"Have you lost your tongue?"

He shook his head, biting his lip.

"Then answer my question, boy. Are you a bad seed too?"

Alfie felt his cheeks burning as Snitch barked at him.

"WELL?"

"No, Miss Snitch," he burst out at last. "And neither was my mum!"

Snitch's face went purple with rage. The buttons on her jacket nearly popped right off as she took a huge breath to blast her wrath down upon Alfie.

"Look out, she's about to blow!" whispered Jimmy.

Just before she could let rip, Murkle scurried over and whispered in her ear. Snitch's chest slowly deflated like a punctured balloon. She straightened her jacket and smiled malevolently down at Alfie. "As this is the first day of the term, and I have a forgiving nature, the punishment for your insolence will be mild."

Alfie began to breathe a sigh of relief, but saw the

frozen expressions of everyone else in the room and realized he had relaxed too soon.

"Before you leave tonight, Mr. Wexford in the woodworking department will provide you with a square piece of board. You are to collect one hundred horse chestnuts. On each of these chestnuts you will *neatly* carve the words, 'I shall not play the court jester while I am a student at Wyrmwald House.' You are to attach each of these reminders of your behavior neatly to the board and present it to us in the morning."

"How am I going to find a hundred chestnuts and do all that in—" began Alfie.

"Silence! Do you want me to make it one thousand?"

Alfie pressed his lips together.

"Very good. Then we will see you tomorrow at nine a.m. sharp."

"You suicidal or something?" breathed Jimmy as the headmistresses marched from the stage. "I can't believe you got a Hall of Penitence punishment on your first day! Sounds like she had it in for your ma, so I'd be careful if I were you. Don't bawl them out in public again. Still, good on ya." He grinned.

Mr. Ramdhay, the music teacher, began to play the piano and led the whole school in singing "Getting to

Know You" from *The King and I*. Alfie scowled at Edward, who was still too busy snickering at his chestnut trick to sing along. *Three enemies in one day*, Alfie thought. That had to be some kind of record.

"I'm never going to find a hundred chestnuts!" sighed Alfie during afternoon break. He flopped to the ground under the horse-chestnut trees and counted out the eleven he had managed to collect with the help of Robin and Jimmy.

"Yeah, you might be right there," said Jimmy unhelpfully.

"Me and Maddie will help you look for more on the way home," said Robin, more encouragingly. But Alfie knew it was unlikely; the kids of the village had pretty much picked the ground under the trees clean. Maybe he could climb up to pick and peel the unripe ones? He didn't like to think about what would happen if he failed in his punishment.

"Hey, Alfie," called Madeleine, rushing over with Holly. "I found these this morning. Thought they might come in handy." She tipped six chestnuts into Alfie's lap.

"You can have mine too," said Holly with a smile, offering up eighteen. "We've got a tree in our garden."

"Thanks, Holly!" said Alfie. "Well, that's just over a third of them."

"That's the spirit," said Jimmy as the bell sounded and they headed to their classes. "If you make it to fifty maybe they'll only half kill you tomorrow."

Alfie was highly relieved when the school bell finally marked the end of his first day at Wyrmwald House. The twins helped him scour the ground for chestnuts on the way home.

"Hey, new kid!" someone shouted. Alfie turned to see a group of older students led by a dark-haired boy. "Billy Reynolds," he introduced himself. "Way to wind up M and S on your first day!"

"Good of you to keep them off everyone else's backs," said the tall, mousy girl behind him.

"Glad you got something positive out of my pain," said Alfie.

"Yeah, well, thought you might like these." Billy handed over a paper bag full of chestnuts. "There's forty-one in there. We've been collecting all afternoon. Loads of people donated."

"That's brilliant, thanks!" said Alfie, touched by the gesture.

"No worries," said Billy. "Maybe your masterpiece will hang next to my old soccer ball. Immortalized in the Hall of Penitence!"

"You're quiet tonight," said his dad as they ate together in the Great Hall. "After dinner, how about helping me work out why water swirls the wrong way down the plugholes here?"

"Sorry, Dad," said Alfie. "I've got a lot of homework and a test tomorrow. I'd better study." He had decided not to tell his dad that he had gotten into trouble on the first day of school.

"A test, already? Good, I'm glad they're keeping you on your toes. Anything I can help with?"

Alfie pulled the school handbook out of his bag and handed it over. His dad's face dropped as he flicked through it.

"It's okay, you're excused," Alfie laughed.

"Right, well I'm going to check out those plugholes," said his dad, clapping his hands, then rubbing them together. "Give me a shout if there's anything on math or science."

At half past nine, Alfie finally took a break, putting down the compass he had been using to painstakingly scratch his lines into each chestnut. He tried to stretch the cramp out of his hands, which felt as though they were turning into claws. "Fifty-nine," he counted as he glued the one he had just finished to the board, almost completing the fifth row of ten. He hoped Amy was having a better time at Hillston Middle School than he was at Wyrmwald House.

A gust of wind blew the shavings from his desk as Artan swept in through the window and landed on Alfie's bed.

"Mmph gu loh," he mumbled before coughing something out onto the bed.

"What was that?" asked Alfie.

"I said, that's the lot," said Artan, proudly nudging the little pile of chestnuts in front of him with his nose. "I could find you another hundred if you like?"

"No, thanks," said Alfie. "That's all I need. Besides"—he gave the bear a weary grin—"any more and I'll go nuts." He nearly jumped out of his skin as Artan roared with laughter. The bear seemed to appreciate hearing puns just as much as making his own.

"Alfie?" called his dad's voice from the hallway.

"Quick, on the floor!" whispered Alfie. Artan slid onto the floor near the fireplace and assumed a frozen open-mouthed expression just as Alfie's dad entered the room.

"Were you laughing at something?"

"Just thinking about something funny that happened at school," said Alfie quickly. He knew his dad would be thrilled by Artan, but would ban him outright from something as dangerous as going on flights with the bear.

"Glad you're enjoying it there," smiled his dad. "But I'm surprised that they gave you so much homework on your first day. What is this anyway?" He started across the room toward the chestnut-covered board.

"Just an art project," said Alfie quickly, snatching the board away before his dad saw the lines carved into the chestnuts. "I don't want anyone to see until it's finished."

"Ah, I can understand that," said his dad, tapping the side of his nose. "Top-secret stuff. Well, ready for bed and lights out in ten minutes. You don't want to be late and get into trouble in your first week."

"Who, me? I'm planning on being a model student," said Alfie, wearing his best innocent face.

"Hmm, you can start at home by keeping your room tidy," said his dad, ruffling his hair. "Well, good night . . ." He stopped on his way out the door, a puzzled expression crossing his face as Artan caught his eye. "I don't remember seeing him before."

"Oh, yeah, I found him in one of the towers," said Alfie. "Just seeing what he looked like in my room."

"I didn't think that would be your kind of thing," said his dad. "A fine beast though. Must have been a king among bears."

"A wise man," said Artan, rippling proudly as soon as the bedroom door clicked closed. "Knows what's what. A king among bears, that's me!"

It was two in the morning by the time Alfie glued the last chestnut to the board and began his second task, studying the school handbook for the test. He finally fell asleep around four, rules, regulations, and chestnuts swimming through his mind.

The next morning, as he wearily dragged himself through the school gates, nervously clutching his punishment,

Alfie was very surprised to see that the other students were lining the route to the school doors. A rhythmic clap began when he appeared. Madeleine and Holly raced up to meet him as he entered the schoolyard.

"They've been waiting for you," said Holly, as the clapping grew faster and louder. "Go on then, hold it up." She pushed his arms up so that he was holding the chestnut-covered board high in the air. The playground rang with resounding applause and whistles. It seemed that getting the first punishment of the year had given him a legendary status at his new school. Alfie held his punishment proudly to his chest like a badge of honor and the students began to chant as he walked down the line toward the school doors.

"AL-FIE, AL-FIE, AL-FIE."

Students patted him on the back and wished him luck as he passed—all except Edward, who didn't look at all happy that his trick to embarrass Alfie had backfired.

Alfie marched up the schools steps and into the cool halls. The jubilation he felt at his warm reception slowly turned to fear as he saw Murkle and Snitch waiting for him outside the Hall of Penitence.

"Quite the welcoming committee," sneered Murkle as Alfie stopped in front of them.

"One might think you were enjoying your punishment," said Snitch, glaring down at Alfie, who shook his head hurriedly. "Well then, hand it over."

Alfie held out the board and waited anxiously while Murkle and Snitch carefully examined his work.

"Shoddy workmanship," sniffed Snitch.

"And the writing, awful," said Murkle.

"Appalling," agreed Snitch. "I have a good mind to ask you to do it again."

Alfie stared dolefully at Murkle and Snitch as it dawned on him that they would never be satisfied with his work. He imagined a whole school year of punishments every single night, each one rejected the next morning by the two crazy headmistresses.

"However," Snitch continued, "as we are in rather a good mood, we will accept this feeble attempt. Although it is hardly worth gracing the spot we have reserved for it."

Alfie looked up in surprise. "Thank you, miss," he stammered, starting to inch away from them. "Can I go now?"

"You may go," said Murkle.

"But remember," hissed Snitch as she glared down at him. "We will be watching you."

Alfie dashed off to his first class, slightly disappointed that he didn't get to see the Hall of Penitence firsthand, but relieved that his punishment was over. If that was Murkle and Snitch in a good mood, he never wanted to see them furious.

CHAPTER ELEVEN

Stakeout

The following weeks passed rather quietly compared to Alfie's first day at Wyrmwald House. He had been very busy with homework but had still managed to share a few more flights with Artan since the trip to London. Fortunately, they hadn't seen any trace of the creatures that had attacked them during summer vacation. Alfie was starting to believe Robin could be right—maybe they had flown too close to an eagle's nest.

October was a hectic time. Lessons and rehearsals for the school play were in full swing, preparations for winter were under way at the Merryweather farm, and the twins' birthday was drawing close. Alfie had to make excuses to avoid them for a few days so that he could finish working on their present. On the morning of their birthday, he presented each of them with his handmade gift over breakfast in the farmhouse kitchen. A first edition of *The Terrific Trio*, a comic he had drawn featuring their recent adventures—or rather the adventures of the Boy Genius, Dynamo Girl, and the Timeslip Kid.

"Look at this, Herb, they're flying over London on a bearskin rug!" laughed Aunt Grace, reading the comics over Robin and Madeleine's shoulders. "You certainly have your dad's imagination, Alfie."

"And your mum's talent," added his dad, giving his shoulder a squeeze. "This artwork is brilliant!"

"Why don't you give them your presents, Dad?" said Alfie.

His dad looked a little embarrassed as he handed two clumsily wrapped packages to the twins.

"I hope you like them. I put them together myself."

Alfie beamed proudly to see the twins' faces light up as they opened their presents. Robin had a pair of brass goggles that looked like a cross between a microscope and binoculars with lots of adjustable lenses. His eyes suddenly appeared far too large for his head as he tried them on and began carefully examining his bacon and eggs.

Alfie helped Madeleine buckle her present around her waist. It was a belt with lots of little pouches containing string, fishing hooks, glow sticks, a first-aid kit, water-purification tablets, a small flashlight, and a pocket-sized survival manual.

"It's an adventurer's utility belt. I, er, thought you might find it useful?"

"I love it, Uncle Will!" said Madeleine, happily investigating the pockets.

"Now you both look just like you've fallen straight out of Alfie's comic," laughed Granny as the twins admired their unique presents.

"Okay, Mum, now what did you and Dad get us?" Madeleine asked cheekily.

"Follow me!" said Uncle Herb. Alfie followed the twins as they raced out of the kitchen after their father, stopping when they reached the oak trees that supported their tree house. Alfie had been kept so busy on the farm over the last few weeks that he hadn't noticed a large tarpaulin draped over the tree house. By the puzzled looks on the twins' faces, they hadn't noticed either. Two ropes hung down from it, and Uncle Herb instructed Robin and Madeleine to take one each.

"Okay, now on the count of three . . . One, two, three, pull!"

The twins pulled on the ropes and the tarpaulin fell away to reveal a completely renovated tree house sitting high among the bird nests in the entwined branches of the two oak trees. There were now two structures linked by rope ladders. The original one had been given a fresh coat of paint and all of the rotten boards and broken windowpanes had been replaced.

Uncle Herb had even built a lookout tower near the top of the trees and fitted solar panels to power a socket and small heater in each room. The rope bridges in between were strung with outdoor lanterns to light the way in the dark. The twins yelled in delight and scrambled up through the branches to explore their new hideaway. Alfie followed hot on their heels. Even though he had his own castle, he couldn't help but feel a little envious of the tree house.

That afternoon, Alfie was pleased to see that nearly everyone in their class had turned up for Madeleine and Robin's party in the barn. The tree house was the subject of much envy. All of the twins' friends demanded to be invited for a sleepover. Alfie was glad that he was automatically top of the list. Holly and Jimmy were the first of the others to receive an invitation to stay at what Madeleine had named Oaktree Lodge.

"It'll have to be next weekend though," announced Robin as Holly and Jimmy groaned with disappointment.

"There are a few things we have to do first." He winked at Alfie and Madeleine. "Tell you later," he whispered.

Granny had set up targets on hay bales and gave the children archery lessons with Madeleine and Robin's old longbows. Alfie was in awe of her skills; she had even competed professionally for a while. She had been training the twins for a few years and they had already won several competitions. At the end of the lesson, the twins put on a demonstration. Their favorite trick was to shoot arrows through apples balanced on the head of their dad's favorite scarecrow.

"Remind us never to upset your cousins," whispered Jimmy as the proud twins rejoined the group with their skewered apples. "Or your gran."

"Why didn't you want Holly and Jimmy to stay tonight?" Alfie asked as the twins finally waved good-bye to the last of the party guests. "It would have been fun to have a sleepover."

"Don't you know what tonight is?" asked Robin. "It's a new moon."

"Of course! Oh, that's perfect!" cried Madeleine.

"Alfie, the rustlers will be out tonight. We can stay in the tree house and keep watch for them."

"You still want to do that?" asked Alfie in surprise. "After what happened to Mrs. Emmett?"

"Yes," said Robin, firmly. "*Especially* after what happened to Mrs. Emmett. She was awful, but we owe it to her to find out exactly who did that to her. We'll be safe if we just stay in the tree house. We can take pictures and pass them on to the police."

Alfie felt very proud of his cousins at that moment. They were prepared to lie in wait for dangerous criminals. All for a woman who had earned them a telling-off for nearly every week of their lives.

"We should ask Artan if he wants to join us," he said with a smile. "He could help scout the area. I'm sure he'd enjoy the adventure."

"Brilliant plan!" said Robin. "I hadn't even thought of that."

That night, Alfie sat in the tree house with his cousins, laying careful plans. Granny and his dad were staying over after the party and it seemed an age before the lights in the farmhouse kitchen finally went out as the adults headed up to bed.

"Right, let's set up."

He wrapped his blanket around his shoulders and climbed up to the lookout, followed by the twins. The lanterns hanging through the branches of the trees looked beautiful in the darkness, but Robin switched them off to make the trees less conspicuous.

Robin set his telescope and camera in front of the window that faced the cattle shed. Alfie blew a few blasts on the whistle to summon Artan. The bear had told him that the whistle would work from anywhere, but he still wasn't sure how that was possible from a mile away. He realized he needn't have worried when there was a loud *floomph* from the roof. Artan's large fuzzy head appeared upside down in one of the windows. "Halloo, young ones. May I join you in your sylvan abode?"

"He means the tree house," said Robin, unable to resist translating. Alfie pulled Artan through the window and helped him prop himself up over a stool. The bear lay with his head on his front paws as Alfie told him about the stakeout.

"No one steals from my friends," he roared. "We'll hunt them down! We'll chase them into the—"

"Shushhhh!" Alfie clamped his hands around the bear's snout and pointed toward the farmhouse. "You'll wake everyone up."

"Sorry!" whispered Artan as quietly as he could manage, which was still quite loud.

Robin had figured out that the animals were always taken between two and four o'clock. To kill time, he had brought a board game he had made himself: Minotaur's Labyrinth. Alfie chose to play as the minotaur while Robin and Madeleine played as Greek heroes. Artan had taken up a lookout position on the roof. Alfie enjoyed hearing the occasional contented *moo* from the cattle shed as they played several games, swapping the role of the minotaur each time.

"Well, that was rubbish," said Madeleine, flipping the board as she lost for the third time in a row. "This is why computer games got invented."

Robin's watch beeped to let them know it was two o'clock.

Alfie was starting to feel cramped in the lookout. "Just popping upstairs for a bit." He clambered outside before Robin could protest, hoisting himself up onto the roof. He lay down on Artan's furry back, resting his chin on the bear's head. "See anything yet?"

"Nothing but bats." Artan rippled a little as he sighed and turned his head toward the shadowy shape of the forest at the foot of the hills. "I remember when those trees spread for miles, across most of this farmland," he said wistfully. "I don't remember much, but I know that I was happy there."

Alfie rolled onto his back and looked up through the branches at the night sky as a warm breeze rustled the leaves around him. It still amazed him that he could see so many stars in the countryside.

"Psssst! Alfie!" hissed Robin from below. "Eyes right."

Alfie looked and saw headlights bobbing across a lane between fields about half a mile away. He zoomed in with his binoculars and described what he could see to his cousins.

"It's an old army-style jeep pulling a horse trailer. There's only one man in it. He's wearing a flat cap, so I can't see his face."

"Okay, false alarm," Robin replied. "It's just Jimmy's dad. He went to pick up some horses from the Lake District after the party."

Alfie watched Mr. Feeney unload two horses, then spend a while getting them settled in their new stable before heading into the house. Ten minutes later the lights went out, and everything was still once again.

It was now half past three in the morning. Alfie was

trying to decide whether or not he needed the toilet enough to make the climb down the tree. He had just about motivated himself when a huge dark shadow swooped down toward the Feeney Farm. He froze. Artan growled softly as it landed silently on top of the stables, paused for a moment, then took off and glided to the roofs of several other outbuildings. Slowly, Alfie reached down, his eyes fixed on the creature as he rapped gently on the side of the lookout.

"What is that?" whispered back Madeleine. "I can't see to photograph it through the branches."

Alfie strained to see through his binoculars but it was too dark. A minute later it was in the air again, sailing within a hundred yards of the trees. He could barely make out its shape, but it was easily as big as an elephant, with batlike wings the size of two hang gliders. It landed silently on the roof of the barn where the sheep and goats were kept, folded its wings, and settled there. What was it? He lay flat and perfectly still, praying it wouldn't come anywhere near the trees.

"Hold on," whispered Artan. "We're going for a closer look." Alfie's stomach lurched, but before he could stop him, Artan had slid silently from the tree house, gliding low to the ground. As they drew close to the outbuildings, he flew upward and landed silently on the steeply pitched roof of the bale shed. They both peered over the ridge at the creature, which seemed to be sniffing around on the roof of the barn, scenting the animals asleep below.

Alfie could just make out the silhouette of its spiny back against the starry night sky. A long whiplike tail snaked up from the roof, slowly swishing from side to side in the same way as Galileo's when he was getting ready to pounce. At the moment it seemed too distracted by the food below to take notice of anything else. It began scratching at the plastic sheeting Uncle Herb had used to patch a hole in the roof. Soon it had torn away the plastic and was dipping its head down into the barn.

Alfie tried to push himself up a little higher with his toes, but only succeeded in dislodging one of the roof tiles. He desperately tried to hold on to it with the tip of his sneaker, but it was made of heavy slate and slid away from him, clattering down the roof before getting caught on the moss. It was the loudest sound he had heard in his entire life.

When he could finally bear to open his eyes, the creature was still and alert, scanning the farmyard for the source of the noise. Alfie lay low, holding his breath as it turned toward the bale shed, then paused as if it knew he was there. Its tail began to swish again and caught the plastic sheeting it had torn up, knocking it down into the barn. The stillness was instantly broken by a goat bleating, and within seconds the whole barn was alive with baaing sheep and goats.

The creature stomped its frustration on the barn roof. Spreading its massive wings, it glared directly over at where Alfie hovered on Artan's back. There was a deep snort and two balls of flame emerged from its nostrils as it reared up on its back legs. Alfie stared, frozen in terror as the beast was lit up in its entirety, batlike wings held high against the sky. Flames glinted in its greenish coppery scales as it raised two enormous heads. Alfie stared in disbelief. The rustler and the creatures that had attacked them in the sky were the same thing: the giant two-headed dragon right in front of him.

He needed to get as far away from it as he possibly could, but Artan seemed to know that it would give chase the second he took flight. As the light of the flame died away, someone in the house switched on the floodlights and the farmyard lit up as bright as day. The dragon let out a low hiss, beat its powerful wings twice, and shot upward into the night, the breeze nearly sweeping Artan from the roof. By the time the adults ran outside in their pajamas it had disappeared from view.

"Quick, head to the trees," Alfie hissed to the bear.

Artan launched himself into the air and swooped down to skim the grass by the oaks. Alfie leapt from his back and began to climb the tree, calling to the bear, "Go back to the castle—I'll see you tomorrow." Artan had only just made himself scarce when Alfie's dad and Aunt Grace ran toward the tree house, calling up to the children. Granny headed for the barn with Uncle Herb, who was gripping his shotgun, ready to confront whatever was disturbing his sheep.

After half an hour helping to calm the animals and secure the barn and outhouses, Alfie was back in the farmhouse kitchen sharing tea and toast as Robin and Madeleine explained what they had seen.

"It was huge," announced Madeleine, "with MASSIVE wings. It flew right over us to our barn. It was as big as a plane!"

"A very *small* plane," Robin interrupted quickly. "It was really big though."

Alfie had also seen his aunt and uncle glance at each other. It was obvious that the adults thought they were exaggerating.

"Could have been an eagle owl," suggested his dad.

"True," said Uncle Herb, rubbing his whiskers. "A friend of mine down in Dunsop Bridge said there's a nesting pair not far from his farm."

"We thought it might be a bird when we first saw it, but it really wasn't!" insisted Madeleine as the conversation turned to how heavy a lamb an eagle owl could carry. "Alfie saw it, didn't you? Tell them it wasn't an owl."

Everyone looked at Alfie. His mouth opened and closed uselessly as he tried to figure out what to say. Telling them that he had seen a two-headed dragon certainly wasn't going to make Madeleine's story any more convincing. He could hardly believe it himself, and he had seen it with his own eyes.

"Tell them what you saw, Alfie," she pleaded. "He saw it up close. He flew over with Artan and they watched it from the roof of the bale shed."

"Flew?" smiled Aunt Grace, pulling Madeleine onto her knee. "And who is Artan, Pumpkin?" Alfie groaned inwardly as he realized what was about to happen.

"He's Alfie's flying bear," said Madeleine, looking up at the adults, who were starting to smile. "He's not a live bear—he's a bearskin rug," she added as her mother began to laugh. "It's true! Stop laughing at me! He flew Alfie over to look at the thing on the roof. It wasn't an eagle owl, was it, Robin? We've seen it before—it chased us on the way back from London. It was a dragon, I'm sure it was!"

Alfie felt helpless as everyone collapsed into full-blown laughter.

"Isn't that the story in Alfie's comic?" asked Aunt Grace. "Is this a preview of the next issue? I wish you were this dedicated to your homework."

Madeleine looked at Alfie and Robin tearfully. Alfie still couldn't think of a single word to help her. He wasn't going to tell them about Artan—he'd never be allowed to fly again. He raised his hands helplessly as Madeleine pushed her way out of her mother's arms and ran out of the kitchen, slamming the door behind her. As the adults wiped their eyes and tried to stop laughing, he heard Madeleine scream in anger and stomp upstairs to her room.

"Well, it's been quite a birthday this year," said Granny, getting up and planting a kiss on each of the boys' foreheads. "I hope you two weren't trying to frighten Madeleine out there. I'd have been scared to see a bird that size at night, never mind a dragon."

The tree house was off-limits for the rest of the night, so Alfie was back in the top bunk bed in Robin's room. As Uncle Herb began to snore in the bedroom next door, he leaned over the edge of his mattress to whisper down to Robin about the dragon on the barn.

"It's just . . . *unbelievable*," said Robin. "That's really what chased us. A dragon. I mean, I've read stories about them that say they died out or were killed by knights, but I never thought they really existed! Where do you think this one came from?"

"Don't ask me," said Alfie. "But remember Granny told us that animals have been disappearing from this area since before her granddad's time? What if it has always nested around here, coming out to steal animals every new moon?"

"For hundreds of years," whispered Robin. "It must have hidden itself well. Why do you think it's being more reckless now?"

"What do you mean?" asked Alfie.

"No one has ever seen any sign of it before, right? It seems weird that we've encountered it twice since the castle reopened and you arrived back in Hexbridge with Orin's magic."

Alfie chewed his lip. Could Robin be right? Dragons

were supposed to be magical creatures. Had it sensed the magic inside him that night in the sky, or was it the castle itself that it was interested in? "Do you think Maddie is asleep? Should we go and tell her?"

"Are you kidding?" asked Robin incredulously. "I'd rather face the dragon! We'll be lucky if she speaks to us again this year, never mind tonight."

Alfie barely heard his cousin; a terrible image had popped into his head that kept him awake long after Robin had drifted off to sleep. As Alfie lay in the top bunk staring up at the ceiling, all he could think about was the blackened patch of earth where they had found Mrs. Emmett's melted glass eye . . .

CHAPTER TWELVE

The Secret in the Cellars

Robin was right. The next morning, Madeleine disappeared to visit Holly. Alfie didn't see her until the following morning at school, where she stayed well away from him and Robin. This continued for the entire week.

"I'm done trying to apologize," said Robin in frustration as Madeleine passed them in the corridor, turning her head sharply to avoid looking at them. An embarrassed Holly shot them an apologetic glance as she hurried along behind her. "What did she expect? We couldn't get a clear picture. How could we back her up with no evidence?"

"What's bothering me is that we can't even do anything about it," said Alfie. "You saw how they all reacted to Madeleine. Imagine if we called the army to tell them there's a dragon loose in Hexbridge!" He twirled his finger by his temple, then stopped as a thought hit him. "It's fall break and my birthday next week. What if she's still upset with us?" They'd planned to explore the castle cellars during their break. He couldn't imagine Madeleine not joining them.

"Don't worry—the village festival starts on your birthday," said Robin. "She loves that. She's bound to come round before then."

By the start of the break, Madeleine was still determinedly avoiding them. Alfie was worried. It really seemed as though she was never going to speak to him again. Robin came up to the castle to visit Alfie on the first night of vacation and told him that Madeleine had moved into the spare room of Granny's cottage.

"She told Mum she needed to be there all week to help Granny with festival duties. Well, she can stay there forever for all I care. I'm staying here."

Alfie didn't mind having Robin around at the castle, as he seemed quite happy to amuse himself reading in the library. He was obviously planning on sticking around for a while, as he had already moved some of his things into the room Alfie had given him.

On the second day of vacation, they spent the morning down at the lake with Alfie's dad. He had been inspired by the da Vinci replicas he had seen in Caspian Bone's office and was trying to re-create some of the artist's inventions, starting with two huge pairs of boatlike shoes designed for walking on water. What Alfie thought was going to be a relaxing morning fishing turned into a very wet few hours testing the shoes. His dad had supplied each of them with two ski poles with floats on the bottom to help them balance.

"It's easy," Alfie heard his dad shout from the shore as his feet shot out from under him, dunking him into the lake for the third time. "Just walk across the surface of the water."

"If it's so easy, why don't you try it?" spluttered Alfie as he tried to stand up.

"I would," replied his dad, tapping the video camera he was using to record their progress. "But I need to observe the strengths and weaknesses of the design."

Alfie thought that the design had more weaknesses than strengths as he wobbled around with Robin. The most either of them could manage was five steps before falling face-first into the water.

Just as he was about to plead with his dad to end the torture, Ashford turned up with warm towels and a hamper of food. Alfie sat draped in his towel eating a steaming freshly baked pie as his dad showed Robin the footage of their disastrous attempts to walk on water in the camera's viewfinder. Alfie turned to grab a napkin from the hamper and noticed a lone figure high on the riverbank. It disappeared almost as soon as he looked, but not before he recognized Madeleine's red jacket.

Ashford took that evening off. He had taken a few days and nights off since starting work at the castle. Alfie wondered where he went on those occasions. He still knew very little about Ashford, and the butler seemed determined to keep it that way, avoiding any personal questions. With no one to make dinner, Alfie's dad ordered pizza before disappearing into his workshop to improve his designs. Alfie was quite relieved Robin wouldn't get to experience his dad's bizarre cooking.

After they'd eaten, Alfie led his cousin down from the kitchens to the levels below. He had decided that tonight they would make a start on exploring the cellars.

At the bottom, Alfie flicked a large brass switch and the torches on the walls flared to life, illuminating the undercroft's vaulted ceilings and columns. He took one of the torches from the wall and looked around. This first chamber was the neatly stocked pantry. Jars of pickles, preserved fruits, chutneys, and marinades filled the shelves, all labeled in Ashford's perfect handwriting.

"Careful," said Alfie as Robin caught his foot on one of the large sacks of fruit and vegetables that lined the wall, sending potatoes rolling across the floor. Alfie unlocked the door that led from the undercroft into the main cellars and they made their way down the corridor, detouring through the network of rooms that led off from it. Alfie sorted through the surprisingly large bunch of cellar keys, matching them to locks as they went. One room was lined with large oak casks labeled as elderberry, elderflower, blackberry, or fruits he hadn't even heard of. He was amazed to see they all still had wine in them. Robin pulled the stopper out of a barrel marked ARMAGNAC, 1402. Alfie laughed as he took a deep sniff of the contents and pretended to faint.

"Blimey, why would anyone drink that stuff?"

Most of the other rooms were empty, containing only benches, tables, and baskets of blankets and fleeces. Like everything else in the castle, they were in perfect condition.

"Orin's letter said that the whole village would move into the castle whenever they needed protection," said Alfie. "I bet this is where some of them slept."

In one room Robin found a small leather pouch containing a whittling knife and a number of little half-carved wooden animals, including a boar, a wolf, and a hare. Alfie let him have these under the finders-keepers rule and enjoyed the delighted look on his cousin's face as he examined the animals one by one, gently brushing away loose wood shavings.

At the far end of the corridor was a heavy studded door with three large padlocks. Alfie unlocked them and hauled the door open. A cool wave of damp-smelling air washed over them. Alfie flicked on his flashlight and picked out a long flight of stairs that led downward.

"What do you think is down there?" asked Robin, his voice echoing back at them.

"Let's find out!" said Alfie, hoping he sounded a lot braver than he felt. He forced himself to move before he had time to chicken out. "Stay close." He was a little disconcerted by their own echoing footsteps as they descended into a dark, mossy labyrinth, which made the cellars they had just left seem cheery by comparison.

"We must be at lake level now," said Robin, as they finally reached the bottom.

There were no lights down here and the glow from Alfie's flashlight only made the blackness seem even darker. He had to be very careful to remember where they had come from and where they had already been.

After what felt like hours searching the dank, dark cellars, they finally found something interesting in one of the farthest corners: a vast round trapdoor set into the floor. An intricate array of bolts ran around the edge of the ebony wood surface, which bore silver runes that spiraled toward the center. They looked immediately familiar to Alfie.

While Robin tried to find a way to pry apart the bolts, Alfie quickly checked his talisman. The runes matched. Hadn't Emily Fortune said that the talisman was also a key? He noticed a small round indentation in the center of the trapdoor and knew that the talisman would fit it perfectly, but something stopped him from trying it out. There was something ominous about this huge door. Someone had obviously gone to a lot of trouble to seal it, so he wasn't going to try and unlock it until he knew exactly what was down there.

"Come on," he said, ushering a protesting Robin away. "It'd take an army to pull that up. We'd better get back upstairs. Dad will be wondering where we are."

As they were passing through what Alfie had worked

out to be the central chamber, Robin stopped moving and shushed him.

"Shh! I just heard something."

Alfie held his breath and listened carefully. A soft *plink-plink* broke the silence. "It's just dripping water," he said with a sigh of relief. "You nearly gave me a heart attack, Rob!"

"Sorry," said Robin as he began walking again. "It's just so creepy down—" He disappeared with a loud splash.

"Robin!" shouted Alfie, his flashlight picking out a round pool of water in the middle of the room. Robin had tripped over the low stone lip and was thrashing around in the dark water, grasping for the sides. Alfie began to laugh, but quickly saw that something was wrong. "Quick, grab my hands!" he shouted as Robin disappeared beneath the surface. He grasped at Robin's flailing arms as he resurfaced spluttering—his fingers closed on Robin's sweater, but his cousin slipped out of it and below the surface. With barely a thought, Alfie kicked off his shoes and leapt into the water, taking a deep breath before diving down. The second he submerged he could feel a strong current dragging him deeper. He scrabbled at the sides but couldn't grip on to the slippery stones as the current pulled him down and around a bend.

Fighting the impulse to breathe, he found himself tumbling toward a rusted iron grate. As he hit the bars, he felt something soft next to him. Robin. His eyes were bulging and bubbles escaped his mouth as he clung to the grate. He gestured toward an area that seemed almost rusted through and began kicking at it frantically. Alfie joined in, stomping the metal as it began to crumble away in large pieces.

Alfie's lungs were screaming for air; he was desperate to give in and take a deep breath, but he kept on kicking. Finally, a large section of grate broke away and Robin shot through the hole like an eel.

The jagged metal scraped Alfie's arms as he dragged himself through and out into what could only be Lake Archelon. Weeds grasped at his ankles as he kicked up toward the surface and swam for his life. He could just make out the light of the moon piercing the murky water and kept kicking toward it. His lungs burned and his waterlogged clothes seemed to be dragging him down. Just as he felt he couldn't take another stroke, he broke the surface next to Robin and took a huge breath of sweet night air.

CHAPTER THIRTEEN

Orin Hopcraft's Study

It had been horrible for Alfie to see his dad turn so pale as they had staggered into the castle dripping wet, covered in scratches from the iron bars and coated in mud after scrambling up the hill. He patched up their scrapes and made it very clear that they were never to go down into the lower cellars on their own again. From the tone of his voice, Alfie knew better than to try and argue.

Granny had called for help with the festival preparations that afternoon. Alfie's dad hadn't told her about their close shave, but sent them straight down to the village hall to be put to work. They found Granny standing amid strings of bunting, directing the men and women of the organizing committee. Alfie watched with admiration as she sent them all about their allocated jobs, painting or renovating props and stages. The hall was a hive of activity.

"About time, boys," she called. "I was about to come and drag you out of bed myself. Now, into the kitchen. You're on pumpkin-carving duty."

Before Alfie could say a word, she had swept them into the big catering kitchen with its huge ovens and tea urns. Every surface was covered in pumpkins of all shapes and sizes. There was a horrified gasp from the far corner and they turned to see Madeleine staring at them amid a sea of stringy pulp and seeds. She leapt up and made a dash for the door but it slammed shut before she was even halfway. She let out a yell and pounded on the door as a key turned loudly in the lock. Seconds later, the serving hatch snapped open and Granny's head popped through, a mischievous glint in her eyes.

"This door won't open until you three sort yourselves out. Madeleine has been driving me crazy, moping around my cottage for days. Hopefully some creative hard work will get you three on good terms again. Drinks and sandwiches are in the fridge. Now, get busy!" The hatch snapped shut.

"What if we need the bathroom?" called Robin.

"Then you'd better make up sooner rather than later," called Granny's distant voice.

"I should have guessed she'd try something like this," said Robin, slumping against a cabinet and picking up a large pumpkin. "She means it—she'll leave us in here all night if she has to."

"What about it, Maddie?" asked Alfie hopefully. "Friends?"

Madeleine continued carving, showing no sign of having heard him. Alfie shrugged helplessly at Robin, then sat down on the floor and got to work on a pumpkin. Robin sighed and joined him.

Halfway through hollowing out his third pumpkin, Robin brought up the subject of the huge sealed door in the lower cellars. As he spoke, Alfie noticed Madeleine slowing down in her work. She didn't look their way, but he could tell she was listening intently.

Alfie pulled the talisman out of his shirt and showed it to Robin. "There's no way I'm opening that thing until I've asked Caspian about it, but I'm sure that this is the key—it matches the markings exactly."

"What if it's something really valuable?" said Robin. "Like gold. Maybe that's what the dragon is after!"

"Do dragons really love gold, or is that just a myth?" said Alfie.

"Until last week we thought dragons were just stories. Who knows what they're really like?"

Alfie had to accept Robin's point. He hardly knew what to believe anymore.

"Do you think it's lonely?" he said as he jabbed two eyes into his pumpkin. "I mean, it must be the last of its kind. I've never heard of anyone else seeing—"

They both jumped as two loud bangs on the counter above interrupted their conversation. Madeleine stood looking down at them, arms folded. Next to her were the two pumpkins she had been carving.

"Here's what's happening," she said sharply. "I'll admit that there wasn't anything you could say to Mum and Dad to make them believe me, so I'm going to forgive you . . ."

"Really?" said Alfie. "That's so big of you, Madeleine, thank—"

"IF," continued Madeleine, "you admit that you were a couple of pigs for not backing me up. Agreed?"

"But you just said that there was nothing we could say," said Robin. Alfie prodded him in the ribs.

"Agreed. We were a couple of pigs," said Alfie, happy that Madeleine was finally talking to them again. "We'll always back you up in the future."

"Well?" Madeleine asked Robin. Alfie gave him another prod.

"Okay," said Robin, looking anywhere but at Madeleine. "Agreed."

"Right, now you're going to tell me everything about the cellars and that thing on the barn—and don't even think about exploring any more of the castle without me. One more thing," she added before Alfie or Robin could say another word. She nodded toward the two pumpkins on the counter, into each of which she had carved a pig snout. "This one is you," she said to Alfie, pointing at a pumpkin with a twisted face, crossed eyes, and buckteeth. "The other one is you," she told Robin. His pumpkin was even uglier.

Alfie stared at the pumpkins in stunned surprise. "Wow," he said finally, looking from the pumpkin to Robin. "She's captured you perfectly." They both burst out laughing; even Madeleine couldn't stop the corners of her mouth from twisting into a smile.

"She's got you just right too," said Robin, turning to Alfie. "If it had a body I wouldn't be able to tell which was the real you."

Alfie picked up a large handful of sloppy pulp and threw it at Robin. He ducked out of the way and it skimmed the top of his head to hit Madeleine square in the chest. With a shriek, she picked up two handfuls of the orange goo and threw them, scoring direct hits on both Alfie and Robin's faces. When Granny opened the door to see what all the noise was about, Alfie and the twins were rolling on the floor laughing, covered from head to toe in pumpkin guts.

"Well, I see you've been busy. Does this mean you're all friends again?"

Alfie looked at Madeleine, eyebrows raised as he fished seeds out of the back of his sweater.

"For now," she said primly as a large glob of pumpkin slid from her head and onto the floor with a splat.

The next morning, Alfie thought his dad was acting strangely as they ate breakfast in the Great Hall. He was fidgeting a lot and seemed to be trying not to grin as they talked about birthday plans for the following day. Alfie had decided it was pointless having a party at the castle, as his birthday was on the opening night of the Samhain festival. The celebrations would be like a party anyway, but with the whole village there.

A tinkling bell broke through their conversation and

they turned to see Ashford standing by the doorway. Once he had their attention, he cleared his throat and said, "Announcing the arrival of Miss Amy Siu."

"Hey, Al," said Amy nonchalantly as she strolled into the room and took a seat at the table as if she'd lived there all her life.

"Amy!" yelled Alfie, amazed to see his best friend suddenly appear in his new home. "When did you get here?"

"I picked her up from the train station late last night," said his dad, looking rather proud of himself. "Amy will be staying with us for a few days."

"You didn't think I'd miss your birthday, did you?" she asked in mock surprise, tucking into the blueberry pancakes Ashford had placed in front of her. "By the way," she added, spraying crumbs across the table, "I wasn't allowed to leave my room last night in case I bumped into you, so I want the full tour as soon as we finish breakfast. This place is awesome!"

Alfie's dad headed into town to pick up some equipment for his workshop while Alfie showed Amy around the castle and filled her in on everything that had happened to him since the move to Hexbridge. He even showed her Orin's letter and could hardly believe how easily she accepted the existence of flying rugs, dragons, druids, and magic—saying simply, "Yeah, well, legends have to come from somewhere."

In the afternoon, Ashford served Alfie and Amy afternoon tea at the table in the library where they were taking a break from exploring to read comics.

"These are even better than Gran's!" said Amy, working her way through the many varieties of sandwiches, cakes, and treats on the cake stand as Ashford poured them cups of blackcurrant juice from a china teapot. "But don't tell her I said that." She cast a sharp glance at Alfie and Ashford.

Ashford winked. "Your secrets are as safe as my own."

"I like him," said Amy as Ashford left the room.

"You don't think there's something a little bit weird about him?" asked Alfie.

"Like what?"

"He was a bit grouchy when he first arrived, and he knew the castle inside out without even being shown around. He can cook anything we want or get anything we need in minutes, and he just seems so . . . well . . . *amused* all of the time!"

Amy looked at him with one eyebrow raised. "So, what? You're worried because he's a really good butler? And since when is being happy a crime?" Alfie shrugged. "Well then, there you go. Now, more importantly, this dragon—what are you going to do about it?"

It was a question that had been bothering Alfie for some time. Who do you tell if you know a dragon is on the loose? Even if he could find someone who would believe it, what could they even do about it? "I have no idea. I thought there might be something in Orin's study on how to banish dragons, but I still haven't found the way in."

"Did you try searching this room?" burped Amy as she got up and looked around. "Makes sense that it would be near the library."

"First place I looked," said Alfie, finishing the last of the cookies. "I tried sliding every single one of the panels and pressed every book in the bookcases, but no luck."

"Maybe that would be too easy. I bet he's testing you to see if you're clever enough to find it. Are you sure there were no other hidden messages on the letter?"

Alfie had already checked the letter a dozen times, but he scanned it once again, with and without the talisman. "Nothing," he sighed.

Amy ran her fingers over the intricately carved panels on the wall around the fireplace. "I bet it's behind here." She set about twisting the lamps and prodding the tiles, but Alfie had already tried them all. If only Orin could give him another clue—or had he already? Alfie looked down at the talisman. Could Orin's letter be a clue to finding the study after all? He put the lens to his eye and scanned the library. Almost immediately a flicker of light from a panel near Amy caught his eye. He rushed toward it to find a small circle drawn on the wood in the same glowing ink as Orin's letter.

"See something?" asked Amy.

"Another message from Orin," said Alfie, sitting back on his heels and examining the images engraved into the panel. The circle had been drawn around the sun, which was indented into the wood. When he looked really closely, he could just about make out some small runic symbols, like the ones on his talisman. "I think it's a kind of keyhole."

"So where's the key?" asked Amy.

Alfie took the talisman from around his neck and pressed it to the indentation. A thrill ran through him as it clicked into place.

"Genius!" cried Amy, as the talisman began to rotate counterclockwise.

After three turns it was released, and the panel swung open before them. Barely hesitating, they stepped through to find themselves in another room lined with shelves. As well as hundreds of books, the shelves held jars of all shapes and sizes containing colored powders, herbs, and dried-up liquids. A large chair sat next to the fireplace. They had found Orin Hopcraft's study. Alfie marveled that there wasn't a speck of dust in sight. It looked as if the druid had just popped out for something, yet the room must have lain empty for hundreds of years.

"Just look at these books," said Amy, reading the titles on the spines. *"A Seer's Guide to Translating Visions, Herbs for Health and Happiness, Egypt's Lost Magicks, Forgotten Beasts of the British Isles, Predicting Plagues and Blizzards with Lizards' Gizzards."* Alfie smiled; he was sure Madeleine would be more impressed with these few shelves than Robin was with the whole library.

On a small desk under the window was a mortar and pestle, along with a number of silver implements for scooping and cutting. On the desk was a note, written in normal ink this time.

Dear Alfie,

*Congratulations on finding my study. I hope
you didn't mind my little test. I knew that you
would pass. In this room are many of my
magical tools and notes, as well as artifacts
and writings I have traveled far and wide
to collect. I hope that they will be of interest to
you, though I must ask that you don't experi-
ment with anything you don't understand.
Which leads me to the seal under the castle—*

Alfie's breath caught in his throat—

*do not attempt to open it. Though it would
require a secret incantation and many horses
to lift it, no chances should be taken.*

*When you come of age at thirteen, I will
offer you instruction in druidic philosophy
and folk magic to help you appreciate these
fruits of my lifelong quest for knowledge.*

*Your friend always,
Orin Hopcraft*

"Aw, man! You inherit a castle *and* you get to learn from a wizard?" said Amy, giving him a shove. "Do you think it'll be some kind of correspondence course? New letters and tests sent every week via this Caspian Bone bloke?"

"A druid, not a wizard," said Alfie, barely registering the last part of the letter, his mind only on the trapdoor. He had thought the letter was going to tell him more about it, but all it had given him was a warning. Orin had called the door a seal. Didn't seals keep things shut inside? What could be sealed beneath his castle?

"Alfie, where are you?" called a very distant voice.

"It's Dad," said Alfie. "Come on, before he finds this place. There's no way he'd let me mess about with this stuff." They shot back into the library and Alfie closed the entrance to the study only seconds before his dad opened the door. He made up his mind to visit again as soon as he had the chance.

CHAPTER FOURTEEN

The Winter King and the Fates

On his birthday Alfie had more presents than he had seen in his life. His favorite was from his dad. He had been wondering about the hammering and sawing noises coming from the workshop for the last couple of weeks. All was revealed when he pulled a sheet off the strange structure that had appeared in the courtyard to discover a wooden raft perched atop plastic barrel floats. There was even a little tent shelter attached to it.

"I was going to give you a new improved pair of da Vinci's boat shoes, but I thought you'd have more fun on the lake with this," his dad said with a smile.

"It's amazing!" said Alfie as he leapt on board.

"You make the coolest presents, Mr. B!" announced Amy. "Permission to come aboard, Captain Al?"

"Granted. Now swab these decks, Sailor Sui!"

Alfie's dad headed off to the village after breakfast.

Many of the adults in the village had been recruited by Granny to set up stalls and decorate the market square, so all of Alfie's school friends were spending the day at the castle. Galileo the cat seemed very happy about the growing pile of wrapping paper and kept diving into it as Alfie opened gift after gift. He had a spy kit from Amy, a homemade board game from Robin, and two high-powered water pistols from Madeleine. When all the presents had been opened, they dragged the raft down to the lake and spent a very soggy morning taking turns to attack and defend it with the water pistols and a big bag of water balloons that Jimmy had brought along.

In the afternoon, Ashford set them to work decorating cakes for the festival. Alfie had partnered with Jimmy and was getting exasperated at the amount of chocolate that ended up in his friend's mouth instead of on their cake.

Alfie noticed that Madeleine was acting a little strangely. She hadn't spoken to him much since he had opened his presents.

"Is Maddie still upset with me?" he asked Robin.

"It's not you. She thinks Amy's amazing, probably because she's from the city. She's trying to act all cool in front of her. Don't mention it, she'll kill me."

Madeleine's unusual appearance suddenly made sense. She was wearing a purple T-shirt with skulls on it, black jeans with a silver chain hanging from the belt, and there were purple extensions clipped into her carefully straightened hair. "Is she actually trying to dress like her?" asked Alfie.

"Yup. She had Holly spend an hour on her hair this morning."

Madeleine obviously sensed someone was talking about her. She pulled a face at them and went back to icing little white skulls onto her cupcakes.

"Hey, I lived in the city too," said Alfie, hitting Jimmy's hand with a spatula as he reached for the chocolate again. "She doesn't worship me."

"Yeah, but you're a geek." Robin stirred some blue food coloring into his icing. "Amy's cool."

"Oh, I see," Alfie grinned. "You luuurve her?"

He ducked quickly as a glob of blue icing sailed over his head.

As it was Halloween, everyone had brought their costumes. Ashford was already wearing his, a black suit and a raven mask with a long crooked beak. Alfie thought that it looked like a strange parody of Caspian Bone, almost as if the butler was poking fun at the lawyer with the costume. He wondered if there was some bad blood between the two.

Alfie still wasn't sure what to dress up as. Most of the others were zombies, pirates, or vampires. Madeleine's costume was a bit more imaginative: She was Little Red Riding Hood wearing a wolf mask. Robin was a mad scientist and Jimmy was his lumbering creation. Amy had brought a black bodysuit with a glow-in-the-dark skeleton printed on it and was painting a skull onto her face to match.

"It's a shame your friend Artan can't come with us," she said, carefully brushing black face paint into her eye sockets.

"Ooh, yes," said Madeleine, "he'd love it so much. Can't he at least hide in a tree and watch?"

"Of course! You're both brilliant." Alfie suddenly realized that his costume had been obvious all along. He raced off to get ready.

That evening, Ashford led the procession of children down the hill. Alfie could sense everyone's excitement as they snaked toward the village, pumpkin lanterns gently lighting the way. Jimmy gleefully told him this was the one day of the year when they could get away with staying up past midnight.

The main topic of conversation on the way was Alfie's shaman costume. He had made a robe out of one of the ancient blankets from the cellar. A gnarled old broom handle had been transformed into a staff, but the crowning glory was his cape. A large bearskin was draped around his back, its claws hanging over his shoulders. Its head rested on top of Alfie's like a hood, casting ominous shadows down onto his painted face.

"It's as if it's looking right at me," gasped Holly. "You look so frightening!"

"Of course he does," said Madeleine proudly. Alfie knew she was really talking about Artan.

Alfie loved Hexbridge village. It was full of old higgledy-piggledy streets and little houses with wooden beams, bulging walls, and wonky windows. Tonight, the entire village was lit with pumpkins and twinkling strings of lights that hung between buildings and lampposts. Lanterns glowed gently on every windowsill around the crowded market square. Warm, familiar smells drifted through the air: toffee apples, toasting pumpkin lids, hog roasts, and cinnamon cider.

"Hey, Alfie!" called his dad, waving them over to the

apple-bobbing barrels he had been put in charge of. "Great costume, son. I bet your furry friend hasn't left the castle in centuries!" Alfie hoped that Artan was managing to keep a straight face.

Alfie had never been much good at apple bobbing, but neither was anyone else. Amy was the only one to grab an apple from the water with her teeth. Alfie's turn didn't last long. After a few seconds he stood up coughing and spluttering, so he was puzzled when everyone burst into applause.

"Very impressive, Alfie," said his dad. "But I think that's breaking the rules. You're supposed to use your own mouth."

Amy snapped a picture as Alfie reached up in surprise to take an apple from between Artan's teeth.

"Costumes don't bob for apples!" he whispered when no one was listening.

"Sorry! Haven't had an apple in years," muttered the bear. "Although I don't think I could stomach one now." Alfie groaned at the terrible joke as they headed toward Gertie Entwhistle's toffee apple and cotton candy stall.

"Don't forget to vote for the Winter King," Granny called as she bustled past with a wheelbarrow full of scrap wood for the bonfire in the center of the square. "The crowning ceremony is at nine o'clock in the village hall."

"What's a Winter King?" Alfie asked his cousins, admiring Gertie Entwhistle's zombie makeup and blood-spattered apron as he paid for their toffee apples (Gertie had an apron for every occasion).

"It's a tradition," said Madeleine. "We crown one every year. He's like the town's lucky mascot until we crown a queen in the summer. Miss Reynard said it's been done for centuries."

"Interesting necklace," said Edward Snoddington as he strolled over with Hugo Pugsley. Both boys were dressed in tuxedos and capes with vampire teeth, and they clearly thought that they looked very sophisticated. "Of course, only new money would flash their gold around."

Alfie looked down to see that the talisman had slipped out of his robe while he was apple bobbing.

"Hey, Noddy, Pug, love the matching outfits," said Jimmy gleefully, earning a scowl from Edward and a shove from Hugo.

"Uh-oh! He shouldn't have done that," Robin whispered to Alfie.

Jimmy gave a yell and shoved Hugo back into Edward. Within seconds, a scuffle broke out between the three boys. Alfie was about to leap in and try to stop the fight when a shout from Amy broke the scrum apart. She was standing between the boys in a mantis-like fighting stance, her hands pointing like hooks toward Edward and Hugo as she fixed them with a cobra's stare. Alfie grinned. The last time he had seen her do this was when Vinnie and Weggis had teased her about living with her gran. Her slightly raised leg twitched as though ready to strike at any moment.

The two boys looked at her for a moment, then appeared to decide that they needed to be somewhere else. Alfie watched as they sauntered casually but quickly in the direction of Edward's mother as she sailed between stalls wearing her usual look of disdain.

"That's right, keep walking," said Amy, following their movement with her hands.

"That was amazing!" said Madeleine, looking at Amy in awe.

"Yes, very good," said Alfie with a smirk. "But you can't pull that act forever. Maybe you should take some lessons before someone calls you on it?"

"No one has tested me yet," said Amy, with a bow.

"Anyway, we've seen so many movies that I'm bound to be awesome. Kung fu is a way of mind."

Alfie rolled his eyes but couldn't help laughing. As he tucked the talisman into his robes, he felt a vibration on the top of his head—Artan was growling. He turned to see Murkle and Snitch at the next stall. They were staring at him, heads tilted thoughtfully. When they realized they had been spotted they did something very strange. They smiled.

"Calm down," whispered Alfie, clasping Artan's front paws in case the bear launched himself at them. "What's gotten into you? They're just the headmistresses at my school." Artan's growl died away as the sisters melted back into the crowd. Alfie couldn't help but feel uneasy at the way they had smiled with their mouths but not their sharp little eyes.

In the center of the square was a dunk tank. Mr. Ramdhay was sitting on the hanging stool mocking the poor aim of the children throwing bean-filled bags at a small target in the hope of dropping him into the water.

"I'd prefer to have a go at dunking Murkle and Snitch," said Alfie after taking his turn.

"I'm not even sure why they're here," said Robin,

watching the two headmistresses slide through the crowd glaring at anyone who brushed against them. "It's not as though they even know how to have fun."

There was a loud splash behind them and a cheer went up from the crowd. They turned to see Madeleine beaming with delight as a very wet Mr. Ramdhay staggered out of the pool.

"At least one of you has a good arm!" he said, wiping water from his eyes. Unfortunately for her, Miss Reynard picked that exact moment to walk past, and she found herself in the middle of a crowd chanting for her to take Mr. Ramdhay's place. "I think I've been relieved of duty," he said as he helped her climb onto the seat. "Don't worry, they're terrible shots."

The village clock struck nine and everyone was ushered into the village hall. On the stage sat a throne made out of a hollowed-out oak stump. Granny stood next to it with a girl not much older than Alfie. He recognized her as one of Jimmy's sisters, Orla. She was wearing a green dress and a wreath of silk flowers that kept slipping down over her eyes.

"As you know, the Samhain festival is one of our village's oldest traditions," announced Granny. "We celebrate the harvest, the end of summer, and the coming of winter. Now, we have one final ceremony. We have counted your votes and our Winter King is . . ." She unfolded a piece of paper and laughed.

"Well, this is very appropriate. For hundreds of years, Hexbridge Castle has been uninhabited. It seems that nearly everyone believes its new owner should be crowned here tonight. Please rise for our Winter King, my grandson, Alfie Bloom!"

Alfie blushed beet red as everyone burst into applause and turned to look at him. As he sidestepped through the crowd toward the stage, his leg caught on something and he pitched forward. He was very grateful to feel a pair of hands grab his shoulders before he fell over in front of everyone. "Thanks," he whispered, then almost jumped with surprise to see his rescuer, Miss Snitch. She was wearing a very satisfied grin as she gave him a large pat on the back.

"Go take your throne . . . Your *Highness.*"

Alfie hurried toward the stage before Artan started growling again. He felt dwarfed by the oak throne as he took his seat in front of everyone.

"Orla Feeney, this year's Summer Queen, will now crown the Winter King," announced Granny as Jimmy's sister stepped forward, pushing her flower crown out of her eyes. The winter crown was a circlet covered with overlapping gilded oak leaves. Gold holly leaves stood upright from it all the way around, making it look very regal. Orla placed the crown on top of Artan's head, and Alfie tried very hard not to pull away as she gave him a quick peck on the cheek to a final cheer from the crowd.

"Now, we dance!" said Granny. She clapped her hands and Mr. Ramdhay took up his fiddle and led the band in a wild ceilidh reel.

Hours later, as they all staggered up the hill to the castle, Alfie announced that it was the best birthday he had ever had. As soon as the adults said good night and disappeared into the Great Hall, Artan floated down from Alfie's back.

"Passengers, take your seats!"

Alfie and the twins laughed to see Amy whooping with delight as Artan flew them up the stairs and along the hallway.

"Thank you for a splendid evening," the bear announced as they hopped off. "You all deserve my best bear hug." With that he wrapped himself around them and squeezed so hard that Alfie couldn't even groan at the pun. Artan flew back to his tower as the gang headed to the library.

"I love the smell of this room," said Amy, taking a deep sniff. Alfie placed his crown on one of the carved griffins for safekeeping and headed for the secret door. He had promised the twins that they could see Orin Hopcraft's study before bed.

Reaching the paneled wall, he heard a quiet *click-clack-whirr, click-clack-whirr* coming from above him. He looked up with a start to see that the carving of the Fates was moving. The noise was coming from their spinning wheel as they weaved, measured, and snipped its threads. They all watched, transfixed, as the little figures began to sing without moving their lips.

We are the sisters Moirae,
though some call us the Fates,
All that live succumb to us,
before they pass the gates.

I am kindly Clotho,
the youngest here by far,
I sit and spin the thread of life
and sing of things that are.

I am fair Lachesis,
by whom your lot is cast,

I measure out the thread of life
and sing of what has passed.

I am feared Atropos,
the one to whom all plea,
I cut the threads and seal your fate.
I sing of what will be.

Many try to cheat us,
but all are doomed to fail,
We favor neither men nor gods,
and always we prevail.

The sisters finished their song and continued with their work. Alfie hesitantly reached up and waved his arm around in front of them. They seemed oblivious to the four children listening below.

"Have they spoken before?" asked Amy.

"No," said Alfie, staring up at the carvings and wondering what was powering the wooden figures. "I've never even seen them move."

"Maybe it's an automaton," said Robin. "Like that mechanical silver swan we saw at Bowes Museum last year."

"I don't think this is clockwork," said Madeleine, balancing on a chair as she examined the carvings. "Besides, those voices were real."

"I know this sounds weird," said Amy, "but did anyone else feel as though they heard the voices in their heads, not their ears?"

Alfie realized Amy was right. It was as though the voices had been inside his head. When Orin's letter mentioned the Fates, Alfie thought he had been talking about some form of divination. The druid must have actually spoken to these very carvings!

Robin started to say something but Alfie shushed him. The youngest of the three women had turned her head toward him and once again he heard her voice in his head.

> *Born before his father,*
> *given craft and curse and hearth,*
> *Upon the child born out of time,*
> *a burden placed at birth.*
> *Once many sought the power*
> *he harbors deep within,*
> *Many failed and many died,*
> *but still it drew them in.*

"What is it?" asked Robin. Alfie put his finger to his lips and cupped his ear to show he was listening. As the voice died away, the second sister began to speak.

> *Others chase his secrets now*
> *and dream of what could be,*
> *Their search is nearly at an end,*
> *tonight they hold the key.*

As she stopped, the eldest woman began her verse.

> *Kin will stand close by his side,*
> *till memories become mist,*
> *Though one foe will be vanquished,*
> *others yet exist.*
> *Good will take up arms again,*
> *an age-old war to fight,*
> *But inner battles must be fought*
> *when magic lends its might.*

"That was weird," said Madeleine as the three women turned back into inanimate carvings. Alfie felt everyone looking at him as he kept repeating the verses under his breath while he searched for something to write on.

"Is that what they said to you?" asked Madeleine, as he found a pen and scribbled down the words he had heard.

"I think this is most of it," said Alfie finally, scratching his neck as he read the words and tried to work out what they meant. Reading the second sister's poem, an icy feeling gripped his stomach. He began searching frantically through his robes.

"What is it?" asked Amy.

"The talisman," cried Alfie in horror. "It's gone!"

CHAPTER FIFTEEN

Fire!

Alfie felt a little guilty that Amy spent the rest of her vacation in Hexbridge scouring the marketplace for the talisman with him, but he had to find it. Even Artan had insisted in joining in on the search, flying out in the middle of the night to scour the hillside and village square, under strict instruction not to let himself be seen. As they helped Granny pack away the last of the festival stalls, Alfie tried to fight the feeling that the talisman was lost for good.

Alfie's dad drove Amy to the train station at the end of the week, singing along loudly to the Beatles as he drummed on the steering wheel. Alfie and Amy sat in the backseat holding a whispered conversation over the scrap of paper onto which Alfie had hastily scribbled down the Fates' strange prophecy.

"That bit there," whispered Amy. "'Others chase his secrets now and dream of what could be. Their search is nearly at an end, tonight they hold the key.' Didn't you say the talisman was a key to the seal you and Robin found in the cellars? What if you didn't lose it? Maybe someone stole it. Someone who wants to open that door!"

Alfie felt as though someone had tipped a bucket of icy water over him.

"What do you think is down there?" she asked, eyes wide. "Did you ask Caspian?"

Alfie shook his head. "No. And I can't ask him now without telling him I've lost the key. What if he takes the castle back? I hated it in the city; I can't go back to how things were there." Amy raised an eyebrow. "I mean, of course I miss you," he said quickly. "But you're all I miss about living there. Things are so great here with Dad. It hasn't been like this since before Mum died." It felt as though his whole wonderful new life was on the verge of crumbling into dust.

At the station, Alfie found it even harder to say good-bye to his friend this time around.

"I hope you find it, Al," said Amy as she climbed on board her train after promising to visit during the Christmas holidays.

"Me too," said Alfie, but he was losing hope.

* * *

The teachers seemed much more relaxed than usual on the first day of school after break. During assembly, Miss Reynard announced that the headmistresses had decided to take their first vacation in twenty-five years. Alfie was sure she was trying to stop herself from joining in when everyone cheered at the top of their voices.

Over the next few weeks the whole atmosphere at Wyrmwald House was much lighter, but Alfie was too tired to appreciate it properly. He wasn't sleeping well. Without the talisman he couldn't even open the study again, and what if he got another letter from Orin but couldn't read it? He even had dreams that the seal below the castle had been opened. Dark shadows were spilling out to drag him down into the earth and he couldn't close it again without the talisman. It didn't help that he kept imagining he could hear giant wings flapping around the castle. He had picked up the phone to call Caspian on three occasions, but the thought of losing the castle and the relationship he had with his dad made him put the phone down without dialing every time.

"I spoke to Artan last night," Alfie told his cousins as they worked on algebra problems at the back of Mrs. Boyd's math class. "He reminded me of something. When I was walking to the stage to be crowned, I tripped and nearly went flying, and Snitch grabbed my arm before I fell."

"That doesn't sound like her," said Robin suspiciously.

"No way," added Madeleine. "She'd love to see any of us fall flat on our faces. So why did she help you?"

"That's what I was wondering. Artan said he saw Murkle stick out her foot and trip me in the first place. He thinks Snitch took the talisman when she pulled me up."

"I wouldn't put anything past them," spat Madeleine.

"Amy thinks whoever took it probably knows it's a key. Remember when they tried to steal plans of the castle from your library?"

"You think they know about the seal?" asked Robin, pretending to write something as Mrs. Boyd passed their way.

"If they took it," whispered Alfie. "And if they did, then they must know what's down there."

There was a cold silence as Robin and Madeleine stared at Alfie.

"No way," said Madeleine, burying her head in her textbook as Mrs. Boyd shot their table a warning glance. "No one has even been in the castle for hundreds of years. How could they know what's down there?"

"I don't know," said Alfie. "But if Murkle and Snitch want it, it can't be good!"

November crept by and still no sign of Murkle and Snitch. Alfie wondered what they were doing. Had they left for good, or were they hiding out in the wing of the school where they lived, plotting ways to sneak into the castle and get at whatever was hidden below the cellars? Artan had offered to fly him out at night to spy on the school, but over the last few weeks more and more animals had been disappearing from farms for miles around. It looked as though the dragon wasn't even waiting for a new moon anymore—it was gorging itself every night, and Alfie didn't want to be in the air at the same time as the beast.

Although Alfie tried to keep up a brave face in front of his dad, he no longer felt as happy and safe in his new home as when they first moved in. He felt like asking his dad if they could move in with Granny, or Aunt Grace and Uncle Herb, at least for a while. Caspian's words kept ringing in his ears—if they ever stopped calling the castle home, it would be sealed forever. Would that happen even if they left for a short while? Did he really want that, when his dad didn't have to worry about money here and had so much time to spend with him?

Alfie was now sure that he wasn't imagining the great wings beating around the castle at night. As he dozed fitfully, he could almost feel the castle's unease. It was alert, as if it knew what was out there. One night as he awoke for the third time, he couldn't take it anymore. He raced out onto the battlements and shouted up at the cloudy moonless sky.

"What do you want? Just leave me *alone!*" The wind whipped his words away into the night sky, which was so cloudy that he couldn't tell whether the shadow disappearing over the hills was real or imagined.

"Alfie?" called a voice from the courtyard just below. "Are you okay?" Ashford was standing on the cobbles, staring up at him concernedly. Alfie made his way down to the butler, briefly wondering what he was doing fully dressed at three in the morning.

"You seem tormented," said Ashford as he sat Alfie at the kitchen table and offered him hot chocolate and a plate of cookies. "Is there anything I can help you with?"

"Just nightmares," said Alfie, as he drank from the steaming mug.

"I've seen you searching for something with your

cousins." His eyes flickered briefly to Alfie's neck, then looked up, as if briefly scrutinizing his face. "Have you lost something? Is that why you can't sleep?"

Alfie kept his face blank. Did Ashford know something about the talisman? "Why, have you found something?"

"No, but maybe I can help if you tell me what you are looking for and where you might have lost it."

"That's okay, it's nothing important." The butler seemed to know more than he was letting on and it was making Alfie uncomfortable. He got to his feet. "I'd better get back to sleep. Thanks for the hot chocolate."

"My pleasure." Ashford's usual broad smile washed back over his face. "If there's anything I can do, you know where to find me."

Alfie darted back upstairs to bed. Until he found the talisman, he couldn't risk putting his trust in anyone—especially someone who seemed to be keeping secrets of his own.

At school, preparations for the play were well under way and Alfie tried to show some excitement about it. Miss Reynard and Mr. Ramdhay had written a musical based on the adventures of King Arthur and the Knights of the Round Table. All the main parts went to older pupils. First years were peasants, pages, or servants, with the exception of Alfie. As he was lending the school props from the castle, it was a unanimous decision that he take on the role of the young Arthur. It was only a small part as squire to Sir Kay, but he did have four words to say and would get to pull Excalibur out of the stone. Jimmy's big brother, Cormac Feeney, would play the main part of the adult King Arthur. Alfie thought Madeleine seemed rather jealous of his role. He wasn't surprised—she was playing serving girl number three and had to spend most of her stage time curtsying to boys.

With the performance only weeks away, Mr. Ramdhay's music and drama lessons had turned into rehearsals and Mrs. Salvador's art classes were taken up with scenery painting and prop making. Today the classes were back-to-back, and Alfie headed straight from rehearsals to the art class they shared with the second years. The art room felt like a medieval junkyard as they worked among castle walls, cardboard trees, and papier-mâché helmets. Alfie was putting the finishing touches to a forest he was painting on the main backdrop when Holly bounced over, beaming.

"You'll NEVER guess what I've just heard! Alice Popplethwaite just told me that Jenny Wheeler told her that Orla Feeney heard Murkle and Snitch got fired, so they stole all the school's money and ran away to France!"

"Really . . . ?" said Alfie, wondering whether or not to celebrate with Holly and Madeleine as they punched the air joyfully.

"Don't believe a word my sister says," said Jimmy. "She's always making stuff up." The two girls' faces dropped.

"Well, at least they're not here now," said Alfie, going back to dotting yellow highlights onto his trees. "I'm pretending they went rafting, got swept out to sea, and had to eat each other." That sent everyone off making up their own reasons for the headmistresses' disappearance, each more gruesome than the last.

Jimmy was in the middle of pretending to be Miss Murkle stuck inside the stomach of a rhinoceros when he looked at his wrist and stopped. "Ah, pants!" He put up his hand to get the teacher's attention. "Mrs. Salvador! I left my watch backstage during rehearsals. Can I go get it?"

"Okay, my dear, but be quick," said Mrs. Salvador as Jimmy raced off to the school hall. "Now everybody gather round so that we can admire your master-pieces."

The class formed a semicircle around Mrs. Salvador, who began pointing out the dents, nicks, and scratches on Ben Carter's papier-mâché sword and shield. "Just look at the attention to detail. This shield looks as though it has seen many fierce battles."

"Jimmy's taking a long time," whispered Robin as the teacher moved on to scenery. Alfie had just been thinking the same. Before he could answer, a shrill bell made everyone jump.

"Okay, poppets, keep calm," said Mrs. Salvador as everyone covered their ears. "That's the fire alarm. Leave your coats and bags, line up and follow me."

"Miss, what about Jimmy?" asked Alfie as they followed her to the nearest fire exit.

"I'll bet he's already outside," said Mrs. Salvador. "I'm sure it's just a drill, but we'll take a roll call once everyone is out of the building."

They were the first class to reach the playground and Jimmy was nowhere to be seen. Alfie looked out for him as the other classes arrived.

"Stop running!" shouted Miss Reynard as her class raced out of the school screaming.

"The hall is on fire!" shouted the boy leading the group. Two girls dashed out behind him, their eyes bright. "The school is burning down!" they yelled.

"Can you see Jimmy?" called Alfie, straining to be heard above the noise. "Did he come back from the hall?"

"He's not here," said Madeleine. "And that was the last class."

"Miss!" Alfie called to Mrs. Salvador. "Jimmy's not here, miss."

"I'm sure he is around, dear," said Mrs. Salvador as she flapped her arms in a futile attempt to herd everyone together. "I'll do the roll call as soon as everyone is in line." Alfie left her rushing around after his classmates, who were running wildly around the playground. He tried to get the attention of another teacher, but they were too busy trying to calm the mob to hear him.

"I'm going to find him," he said, heading back toward the school.

"No, Alfie, it could be dangerous," said Robin, pulling him back by the sleeve.

"Mrs. Salvador said it's just a drill. They're just being stupid—I bet there's not really a fire." He slipped out of his cousin's grasp and motioned him back toward the group. "Cover for me when they do the roll call. I'll see you back in class." With that, he made the most of the chaos to sneak back into the school unseen.

Alfie's pounding footsteps echoed back at him as he ran toward the school hall. He had never heard the place so quiet—there was always a hum of activity from the classrooms, even when the corridors were empty. He hadn't really believed himself when he told Robin that there was nothing to be worried about. Nearing the school hall, he caught the smell of smoke and his fears were confirmed.

He swung open the doors to the hall and was hit by a wall of heat. A thick cloud of smoke billowed around him. Through it he could just make out orange flames licking up the stage curtains at the far end of the hall.

"Jimmy!" he called over the crackling of the fire. "Are you there?" There was a loud crash as one of the lighting rigs fell from the ceiling onto the stage, splintering the floorboards. As the bulbs shattered, he heard a yell from the wings of the stage.

Alfie stood frozen in the doorway, one foot still in the corridor as he frantically wondered what to do. The fire was spreading fast. If he went back to get the teachers they might not get to Jimmy in time. He took a deep breath as he made his decision. Tying his sweater around the lower part of his face, he grabbed a fire extinguisher and fought his way through the smoke, calling out Jimmy's name. A sudden sharp stab of pins and needles prickled all over his body as he dodged around the pools of flame that spattered the hall. What could have caused a fire like this?

The prickling sensation got worse as he climbed onto the stage. As a strip of burning curtain dropped in front of him, something thumped in his chest, and he felt a painful jolt shoot down his arms into his hands, where white sparks crackled like electricity under his fingernails. It felt as though something inside him was trying to get out. Could it be the magic? Was it trying to help him? He could almost feel it inside as he staggered on through the smoke: a churning power with a keen hunger.

"Jimmy!" he yelled again.

"Alfie!" called Jimmy's voice from the wings. "Over here. I can't get through the flames!"

"I'm trying to get to you," called Alfie, following the noise of his friend coughing. "Try not to breathe the smoke!" He kept catching glimpses of Jimmy through the wall of flames—he was holding up a sheet of canvas to try and shield himself from the heat. Alfie reeled back as the flames flared higher, as if he were in the world's largest oven. Another insistent jolt shot through his arms, making his fingers tingle. "Stop it! I don't know what you want me to do!" he shouted over a buzzing that sounded like a hive of bees inside his head.

"I've got a fire extinguisher," he called to Jimmy. "I don't think it'll do much—so you've got to be ready to run." He prayed Jimmy heard him as he pressed the trigger and staggered forward, using the foam to clear a narrow path through the flames.

"Okay, get ready," he called as he battled to keep the route through the fire open. "Now, Jimmy, RUN!" As the last of foam dripped from the extinguisher, Jimmy burst through the flames with the canvas wrapped tightly around him. Alfie pulled him to his feet and they staggered from the stage, struggling to breathe as the thick smoke threatened to fill their lungs.

There was a loud crack above them. Alfie looked up as the curtain rail gave way and the heavy flaming stage curtains slid down toward them. He leapt off the stage, dragging Jimmy with him and rolling out of the way as the vast blanket of burning velvet landed right behind them. Alfie screamed out in pain as his whole body jolted and the buzzing in his head became unbearable.

As Jimmy tried to pull him to his feet, the doors suddenly burst open. Men in face masks and helmets charged into the room, calling instructions to one another as they arranged hoses and started to tackle the blaze. Before Alfie could even call out, he was picked up and thrown across the shoulder of a fireman who rushed him out of the building as steam and smoke billowed down the hallway behind them.

Alfie took deep breaths through the oxygen mask over his face as he sat in the ambulance wondering what had happened to him in the hall. Had the magic been trying to get him to use it, or was it out of control? He remembered the intense hunger he had sensed, as if it wanted to feed on the flames. He watched the paramedic apply butterfly stitches to a cut above Jimmy's eye. Madeleine, Robin, and all of Jimmy's brothers and sisters were crowded around the open doors.

"Are they going to be okay?" asked Sinéad Feeney, Jimmy's oldest sister.

"They'll be fine," said the paramedic. "Although this one will have a nice little scar through his eyebrow." Alfie thought Jimmy perked up quite a bit when he heard this.

"Did you see how the fire started, Jimmy?" he asked, lowering his mask.

"No idea, but it was bloody quick. I found my watch and was putting it on when I heard someone moving around in the hall. I poked my head through the curtains to see who it was and suddenly I was surrounded by flames, like someone was using a flamethrower! Thanks for coming to get me, mate, but you're a total idiot."

"I'll say!" said Miss Reynard, appearing at the ambulance doors. Alfie had never seen her angry before. "The firemen were on their way and we asked you all to wait outside for your own safety. Alfie Bloom, by going back into the school, you not only endangered yourself but also created another person to be rescued. It was extremely foolish of you." Alfie had to look away from his teacher's stern green eyes as she stared gravely at him.

"He is the Winter King, miss," laughed Edward Snoddington, hurrying over to enjoy the show.

"Yeah, miss. He probably thought he could put the flames out with his ice powers," added Hugo with a snort.

Alfie's face felt even hotter than it had among the flames.

"That's enough from you two," snapped Miss Reynard. Her face softened as she turned back to Alfie and Jimmy sitting shamefaced in the ambulance. "Foolishness aside, I am very glad to see you both safe. The firemen told me that they might not have reached Jimmy in time if you hadn't gotten him away from the flames. The entire stage and much of the hall has been destroyed. You were both very lucky."

Jimmy's sisters cried out in alarm when they heard this and leapt into the ambulance to smother their brother with hugs and kisses. His older brothers heaped their gratitude on a sheepish Alfie as he watched the two hecklers drift away, obviously disappointed at their entertainment being cut short.

Miss Reynard turned to Alfie and said quietly, "I can't condone your actions, and it was very wrong of you to rush in there, but . . ." Her eyes twinkled as she treated him to a dazzling smile. "Well done, Alfie. Very well done indeed." Alfie's stomach did a little leap at the unexpected praise from his favorite teacher as she rushed off to reassure the frantic parents who were starting to turn up at the gates.

The school wasn't closed for long, much to everyone's disappointment. Only the main hall had been damaged by the fire. Alfie and Jimmy hadn't suffered more than a few scratches and sore throats from the smoke, so by the time the school reopened they were declared perfectly well enough to join their classmates. However, Miss Reynard had told Alfie's dad what had happened during the fire, and he had been grounded for the foreseeable future. His dad had never spoken to him so sternly before, but what had upset Alfie most was seeing the worry hidden behind the anger. He had made Alfie promise never to do anything so dangerous and impetuous again. Alfie had to admit that he had been let off lightly; he knew how stupid he had been. Guilt still squirmed in his stomach as he hoped he could keep his promise.

Although the whole building had been well aired, it still smelled strongly from the fire. It reminded Alfie of the smells that sometimes wafted from his dad's workshop. The hall had been made safe so that work could begin on the fire-damaged areas, but it was off-limits to the pupils. It was obvious that it would take months to rebuild the stage and repair the rest of the damage.

That afternoon, Alfie sat shoulder to shoulder with the other pupils as they crammed into the small dining hall for assembly.

"As we won't have a main hall for a few months,

things will have to be a little cosier for a while," said Miss Reynard. She had been leading assembly during the headmistresses' mysterious absence, and it was a lot less daunting now that no one had to worry about being singled out by Murkle and Snitch. However, Alfie could see that everyone was a little on edge today. They were expecting bad news.

"I know you were all looking forward to the school play . . ." Alfie groaned along with the rest of the gathered pupils as everyone gloomily predicted Miss Reynard's next words. "But, as you know, we no longer have anywhere to perform. So it is with great regret that we have decided to cancel the play this year."

Dozens of voices called out in protest at the news, particularly from pupils with major parts.

"That's not fair!" called one of the older students. "We've been rehearsing for months."

"And all the props and costumes are safe in the art rooms," added another. "We spent ages making them!"

Someone behind Alfie started shouting about how unfair it was that the hall had burned down before the play rather than during exam time, and suddenly everyone was shouting and pleading for the play to go ahead. As the teachers tried to calm everyone down, Alfie had a brilliant idea. He rushed over to Miss Reynard and could see Madeleine and Robin straining to hear what he was whispering to her.

"Okay, everyone, settle down," called Miss Reynard as Alfie went back to his seat. "Quiet, please!" Mr. Ramdhay finally caught their attention by playing loud dramatic chords on the piano.

"Alfie Bloom has just made the school a very generous offer." The squabbling died down as everyone shushed one another to listen to Miss Reynard. "If everyone still wants the school musical to take place before Christmas"—a couple of whoops went up from the back of the hall—"Alfie has offered to let us use the Great Hall in Hexbridge Castle." At this a massive cheer went around the room.

"All in favor of performing at the castle next month, raise your hands." Nearly every hand in the hall shot into the air—the only two that didn't were those of Edward and Hugo as they scowled through the applause and whistles that filled the room.

"Such a very kind offer," said someone from the back of the hall.

A shiver ran down Alfie's back as he recognized the razor-sharp voice. He could feel the joy draining out of the room. Murkle and Snitch were back.

"An offer we are very grateful to accept, as the school appears to have been partly destroyed in our absence," sneered Snitch.

"Miss Murkle, Miss Snitch," said Miss Reynard, clearly as surprised at their arrival as the pupils who were suddenly trying to sit as upright as possible. "I didn't realize you were coming back today."

"I'd say it's fortunate that we have," snapped Snitch.

"Otherwise there might not have been a school left for us to return to," added Murkle. The two women were clearly enjoying catching everyone off guard. They strode proudly to the front of the room, sweeping Miss Reynard aside. Alfie stared up at them in dismay. They looked even bigger and more dangerous than he remembered.

"It appears that standards have slipped over the past few weeks!" announced Snitch as everyone in the room redoubled their efforts to look like model pupils. Then she said something Alfie found very surprising. "Not to worry. We'll whip everything back into shape in no time. However, young Alfred's most generous offer has certainly lined our clouds with silver." She flashed a smile at the gathered children. Alfie found himself flinching in astonishment with the others—it was obvious that no one quite knew how to react to Snitch being nice.

"Let's hear three cheers for Alfie Bloom!" Murkle beamed.

"What the . . . ?" burst out Madeleine in amazement as the whole hall hip-hip-hoorayed. "Do you think they had personality transplants while they were away?"

"I don't know," said Alfie, unsettled as he looked at Murkle and Snitch's smiling faces. "But I'm starting to think I've just done another very stupid thing."

CHAPTER SIXTEEN

Beyond the Hall
of Penitence

Murkle and Snitch were behaving like different people since their return, and it was making Alfie very suspicious. They weren't exactly nice, but now they were only dishing out detention for *real* rather than *imagined* rule breaking. Even their punishments had lost their edge. Jenny Wheeler had dropped a can of lemonade in the hallway and had been made to clean all of the corridors, but only those on the ground floor of the building.

"The weirdest thing," she told Alfie incredulously as they studied maps of tectonic plates in Mrs. Shoebottom's geography class, "was that they gave me a mop. I expected a toothbrush!"

The headmistresses were also taking quite an interest in the school musical and had even turned up to rehearsals. Robin swore that he had heard them singing one of the songs as he passed their office window.

"It's because you've given them an easy way in, isn't

it?" said Madeleine that weekend as they sat on Alfie's raft skipping stones across the lake. "That's why they're so happy."

"I think so," said Alfie as he glumly watched his third stone disappear without a single bounce. "But that's not what's really bothering me."

"What is it?" asked Robin, giving up on the stone skipping as Madeleine counted her seventh bounce.

"If they're so happy about getting an invite to the castle, who do you think arranged the fire?" The twins stared at him as the terrible realization dawned on them too. "They set the fire while they were supposedly on vacation . . ."

"So no one would point the finger at them," finished Madeleine. "Of course!"

"We're only guessing here," said Robin. "There's no real proof."

"Then we need to find it," said Alfie. "They've got the talisman, I know it. And I'm going to take it back."

Over the next few days, Alfie and the twins watched out for Murkle and Snitch and marked down everywhere they went and when. The only regular pattern he could see was at lunchtime when they collected their luxury steak dinners from the kitchens and took them to the staff room, where they spent at least thirty minutes before returning to their office.

"No wonder all the other teachers eat in the cafeteria with us," said Robin as he watched the headmistresses disappear into the staff room with their trays and set his watch to time them. Alfie led the way to the headmistresses' office, but he couldn't even get into the Hall of Penitence. The doors were firmly locked.

"Well, it was worth a try," said Madeleine, rattling the door handles.

"We're not done yet," said Alfie.

"It's no good. We can't get in without the keys."

"Exactly." Alfie grinned. He had noticed that Murkle and Snitch always carried their keys on them—Snitch on a long chain that hung around her neck, and Murkle on a cord that ran from her belt to her cardigan pocket. He had decided that Murkle's keys would be the easiest to steal and had been looking for his chance to get close to her.

An unexpected opportunity arose on Friday afternoon as the bell rang for lunch. Alfie was on his way from a double history class to the cafeteria when he saw

Murkle screaming at a second year boy who had accidentally stepped on the back of her shoe. Snitch had marched on ahead to get her lunch. Alfie noticed the janitor's wheeled mop bucket in the nearby stairwell and nipped behind Murkle, unable to believe his luck.

Inch by inch, he wheeled the bucket out behind her. He winced as the wheels let out a little squeak, but Murkle was yelling too loudly to hear a thing. Over the shoulder of the quaking boy, he saw Madeleine and Robin coming toward him. Robin's mouth had opened into a shocked little O as he saw what Alfie was doing. He quickly slid the bucket into place and rushed to meet them.

"Hey, Rob, Mads—coming for lunch?" Murkle was too busy screaming to even notice him.

"Alfie, what were you—" began Robin.

"It's liver and onions today. Smells good," he said loudly, cutting Robin off. Murkle had finished her tirade and was watching the boy scuttle away. She gave Alfie and the twins a narrow-eyed glare, then spun around to march into the hall, tripping straight over the bucket and landing in a very untidy wet heap on the floor.

"Miss Murkle!" cried Alfie in mock horror as he ran toward her. "I can't believe that was just left there. Come and help me!" he called to Madeleine and Robin as he tried to pull Murkle to her feet. The twins reluctantly ran over to help. "Are you okay, miss?" he asked as they finally got her up. Murkle snorted at them furiously, her nostrils flaring as she seemed to oscillate between embarrassment and fury. Finally, she shook her hands free and charged away into the school hall.

"I saw that," said Edward from the stairs. "You tripped her over on purpose."

"Looked like she tripped all on her own to me," said Robin.

"I saw *him* move the bucket," sneered Edward, nodding toward Alfie.

"So what are you going to do, tell her?" asked Alfie.

"Maybe," said Edward, a sly smirk playing around the corners of his mouth.

"Really?" Madeleine moved almost nose to nose with Edward, glaring him down. "In the mood she's in?" Edward didn't look so sure of himself anymore.

"Got a photo to prove it?" asked Alfie.

Eventually Edward backed down with a snort. "Maybe I won't bother. You seemed to enjoy the last punishment too much—bet you're just trying to be some kind of school hero again. Who cares what you do anyway?" He stalked off into the cafeteria without looking back.

"What did you do that for?" exploded Robin. "We're supposed to be watching Murkle and Snitch, not winding them up!" Alfie made sure Edward was out of sight, then grabbed the twins' arms and pulled them into the stairwell.

"Look," he said, holding up a cord and swinging two iron keys in front of them like a pendulum. "I swiped them when we were helping her up."

"Oh, Alfie, you're brilliant," laughed Madeleine. "You got it exactly the same way they took the talisman from you." Alfie let her snatch the keys from his hand, his pulse racing as he wondered if he really dared use them.

"You're not suggesting we sneak into their office right now to search for the talisman, are you?" asked Robin incredulously.

"No," said Alfie quickly. "I'm going in alone. I don't want you two risking your necks too."

"That's exactly what we're going to do," said Madeleine immediately. "Now, before you say anything, we've got at least thirty minutes while they eat lunch. If all three of us search together we'll be in and out in no time." She darted out of the stairwell. "Well . . . ? Are we going to get it back or not?"

Alfie didn't have the time to even try to talk Madeleine down. He raced after her, glancing back at Robin, who seemed to be trying to calculate if there was any chance the plan wouldn't end in disaster. His cousin finally let out an exasperated sigh and followed them to the Doors of Doom.

The Hall of Penitence was quite a shock to Alfie as they entered the corridor that led to Murkle and Snitch's office. He had almost dismissed it as legend. The walls were covered from floor to ceiling in hundreds of bizarre punishments, including Billy Reynolds's soccer-ball necklace.

"This is crazy," said Robin, examining a pair of dainty Victorian boots mounted on the wall over a plaque that read: EMILIE WINTERTON. ONE-INCH HEELS. Tiny words were scratched into the leather in neat lines that swirled around the boots covering them completely:

NEVER AGAIN WILL I FLAUNT THE FAIR AND JUST RULES OF WYRMWALD HOUSE BY CRAVING MORE HEIGHT THAN I DESERVE.

"Look at this!" said Robin in amazement. "Murkle and Snitch are just carrying out a tradition. Head teachers must have been doing this since the school opened."

"Hey, look, here's yours, Alfie," said Madeleine. Alfie barely heard—he was too busy staring at the punishment next to it. His heart leapt as he read the plaque below a beautiful hand-embroidered image of the school in brightly colored wool. It read: JENNIFER MERRYWEATHER. INAPPROPRIATE SCHOOL ATTIRE. Staring at his mother's punishment, he recognized the bright colors from a cardigan he had seen in an old photograph of her. Murkle and Snitch must have made her unravel the whole thing. He realized that they couldn't have taken too much pleasure in this trophy. It was so pretty to look at that it cheered up everything on the wall around it. He was proud that his own punishment sat right next to it on the wall. He ran his finger over the embroidery and whispered proudly, "Well done, Mum."

"Alfie, come on," called Madeleine as she swung open the heavy paneled door to the office.

Alfie's heart was in his mouth as Madeleine locked the door and they looked around the daunting office with its ancient wallpaper, surly grandfather clock, and dark wooden furniture. Flames crackled and spat in the large blackened fireplace. The room had a strong smell: a combination of leather, burnt wood, and furniture polish that would have been almost comforting if it wasn't for a rotten undercurrent. Alfie noticed a small stool in front of the huge desk and imagined the fear of every student who had ever sat on it. They had to face two sets of head-mistresses: the real Murkle and Snitch, and the glowering portraits on the wall behind them. They huddled in the center of the room, wondering where to start searching. Even Madeleine seemed too nervous to touch anything.

"Okay, we need to be quick about this," said Alfie, taking charge. "They'll be about thirty minutes, but I don't want to be in here for more than ten. Maddie, you check the cabinets, Robin, you look for a safe, and I'll check the desk drawers and files. Make sure you leave everything exactly as you found it or they'll know some-one was here."

Everyone leapt into action. Alfie began going through each of the desk drawers, carefully removing items, then putting them back exactly where he found them. Robin sent generations of spiders scurrying from their homes as he looked under the portraits, while Madeleine carefully searched through the contents of the glass-fronted cabi-nets. The headmistresses had quite a hoard of strange and disturbing objects, from statuettes and ornate jars to a dusty shrunken head that sat on one of the shelves watching their every move.

"Look at this!" Madeleine called as she staggered over with an enormous scrapbook. She held it out to Alfie. "News articles going back to the 1800s. They're about the rustlers and sightings of a strange creature in the skies over the northeast. It's the dragon! They've collected everything ever written about it. They know that's what has been taking the animals!" Alfie took the book and leafed through page after page of articles on missing animals, strange fires, and incidents across the region, including Mrs. Emmett's disappearance.

"It's all here! Everything the dragon has done. How do they know?" He paused and looked at the others. "And why are they so interested in it?"

"This might sound crazy," said Robin slowly, "but what if dragons are a bit like dogs? What if they need a master?"

There was a cold silence.

"You don't think . . . they're controlling it?" asked Alfie, hardly daring to consider the possibility.

"No way," said Madeleine. "Even if they wanted to, how could they possibly control something like that?"

"Jimmy seems to think they've got some kind of hypnotic power over everyone's parents, so why not dragons?"

Alfie's mind reeled at the terrible possibility. But why would Murkle and Snitch even *want* to control a dragon? Then he remembered the great wings flapping around the castle at night and Robin's idea didn't sound quite so crazy. Had they been trying to use the dragon to find a way into the castle?

"We've got to take this and show Mum and Dad," said Madeleine, grabbing the scrapbook.

"We can't," said Robin, trying to pull the book from her hands. "They'd know we had it, and besides, what does it even prove? That they're interested in strange events?"

Alfie tried to push Robin's theory to the back of his mind as he took the book from the twins and shoved it back into the cabinet. "Come on, we don't have time for this. Let's keep looking."

As his cousins sprang back into action, Alfie sat down on one of the thronelike chairs at the enormous desk and went back to searching through the piles of folders and papers inside. He leapt back as he finally opened the last drawer. It was filled with meaty bones like the ones Uncle Herb fed to his sheepdogs. *Dragon snacks?* Surely they weren't keeping it anywhere nearby? Slamming the drawer shut, he rested his elbows on the desk, hands clasped over his head. They weren't going to find the talisman. Murkle and Snitch probably carried it around with them and he had just missed a perfect chance to check Murkle's pockets. They had been in the office too long already—they would just have to think of another plan.

Alfie stood up to call off the search, but something drew him back. It was as though the talisman was calling to him. He stared down at the desk in frustration. He had been through all of the drawers and even searched underneath them for secret compartments. He ran his fingers over the dark marquetry pattern on the desktop. It was actually quite beautiful for something that belonged to Murkle and Snitch. As his hand passed over the rectangular pattern in the center, a familiar warmth ran through his fingers—the talisman. It had to be under the panel. He began digging around with his nails, looking for a way to pry it up. The ticking of the clock seemed to be getting louder as time passed but the panel wouldn't budge. Less than ten minutes and Murkle and Snitch would be back. "Why won't you *open?*" he shouted, banging his fist down on the desk in frustration. With a little *click*, the patterned panel popped open and Alfie laughed with relief to see the talisman sitting inside on a little pile of papers.

"Hey, come and look at this," said Robin's slightly muffled voice from behind him. He had unlocked the narrow door and crawled partway inside the clock. Only his bottom and feet were visible. "This is so weird—"

"Come out, Robin, I've found it!" said Alfie, fastening the talisman back around his neck.

"Well done!" said Madeleine, joining him and rummaging through the rest of the folder. "They're going to be so mad, but it's not like they can admit they stole it."

"I really think you two should see this," called Robin. His voice sounded strangely distant as Alfie tried to stop Madeleine pulling everything out of the compartment in the desk.

"Hey, look what else is in here." She pulled out a handful of photographs. "They must have taken these at the castle before we caught them snooping around."

Alfie stared. The photos were of the maps Miss Reynard had taken from the headmistresses during the castle-warming party. Various areas of the cellars were

circled on the photos and covered with illegible notes
and question marks. Alfie's blood turned to ice. They
had been doing some research during their little vacation. "We were right," he gasped. "They know it's a key
and they really do want to open the trapdoor."

"Robin!" called Madeleine. "Come and see this!"

Alfie looked around for Robin. Suddenly the door
handle rattled loudly and he nearly jumped out of his
skin. Madeleine grabbed his arm.

"It's them!" she cried.

"What do you mean you can't find your key?" snapped
Snitch's voice from the hallway. "I told you to keep it on
a chain around your neck. Use mine."

Alfie crammed everything back into the folder as
Madeleine searched frantically for a hiding place. He
could hear a foot tapping impatiently on the stone floor
as a key jangled in the lock.

"It won't work—something is stuck in the lock."

"Hurry," snapped Snitch. "That Snoddington brat
said that the Bloom boy and his cousins were hanging
around here. Maybe they took your key."

Edward, that little tattletale! Alfie watched in dread
as the key Madeleine had left in the door started to wobble out of the lock.

Heart thumping against his ribs, he looked quickly around the room. There was nothing that could conceal three children.

"Where's Robin?" he whispered.

"Here," hissed a voice from the grandfather clock. Alfie whipped around to see Robin's head poking around the door at knee level. "Get in, quick!"

"There's no room. We've got to get out of here!" whispered Madeleine, pushing desperately at the locked windows.

"Just get in here!" said Robin urgently. "They'll have the door open any second!"

Madeleine ran toward the clock as Alfie grabbed the photos from the folder before putting it back on the pile. "Alfie, hurry!"

Without thinking, Alfie flung the photos onto the fire and dashed for the clock as they began to curl up and burn. Robin clicked the door closed behind him with barely a second to spare as Murkle's key dropped out of the lock and onto the floor.

It was pitch black inside the clock. Alfie reached out his arms and realized that the space was many times larger than he had expected.

"Watch out for the drop," whispered Robin, guiding

his hands to a set of iron rungs set into the wall. "Quick, climb down, it's not far." Alfie hurried down the ladder, trying not to shout out as Madeleine stepped on his fingers. It was only a couple of yards to the bottom.

"They'll see the key and know we've been in there," said Robin. "We've got to keep moving." At that very moment, Alfie heard the office door bang open, and Murkle and Snitch's voices filled the room above.

"Moving where?" asked Alfie, trying to follow the sound of Robin's voice.

"This way." Robin clicked on the little flashlight he carried on his key chain and raced ahead down the long stone corridor. Alfie dashed after the bobbing light from the flashlight.

"Where does this lead?" he asked breathlessly as he caught up with his cousins.

"I'm not sure. We're heading upward so I guess it leads into the hills behind the school."

The two boys jerked to a halt as Madeleine grabbed their sweaters. "Listen!" she whispered hoarsely. "They're in the tunnel too." Alfie froze and listened.

"We know you're in there!" Murkle's voice echoed up the passageway, making Alfie's skin prickle. "This isn't a safe place for children. We're not cross with you. Come out now and we won't say another word about it."

"Yeah, right," muttered Alfie.

"You don't want to be lost forever in these cold dark tunnels," added Snitch. "Living with the bats, the rats, and whatever else lurks down here in the dark."

Alfie shuddered as he looked into the blackness beyond the light from Robin's flashlight. Every scary film he'd ever watched replayed in his mind. A distant scrabbling noise was coming from far behind them. "They're coming after us!" he cried.

"Run!" shouted Madeleine, sprinting ahead into the darkness.

"Maddie, wait!" called Robin, not bothering to whisper anymore. "Stop running, we need to hide."

"There's nowhere you can hide from us," called Murkle.

"Not in these caves," shouted Snitch.

The noises behind them turned into advancing footsteps. As Madeleine ran blindly into the tunnels, Alfie and Robin realized that they didn't have a choice. They began to run too.

The tunnel started to wind steeply upward as Alfie hurtled through the darkness. The ground became uneven and slippery beneath his feet. He felt cold drafts from either side and wondered if there were other tunnels leading into this one.

"We're in the caves now," panted Robin as if reading his mind. "Granny said they're like a labyrinth under the hills. We need to stay on this path."

Alfie could just faintly hear Madeleine's footsteps in the distance as they ran as fast as they could, their footfalls echoing wetly as the tunnel became damp and more cavernous.

"Do you even know where you are going?" echoed Snitch's voice from nowhere near far enough behind. "I wouldn't run if I were you."

"At least you won't be lonely," cackled Murkle. "Plenty of others have gone missing in here."

"Ignore them," gasped Alfie, "they're just—*Aaaargh!*" His foot caught on something and he fell to the ground, slamming his head so hard his ears began to ring. He felt as if he were underwater as he staggered to his feet, staring dazedly at the thing he had tripped on: a huge cattle skull. A hand grabbed his arm and Robin's muffled voice begged him to move. The air in front of him seemed hazy as he stumbled forward, half held up by his cousin. Something wet was running down his cheek. Water? Or blood? He was jolted to a halt as Robin stopped running.

"I can't hear Madeleine," he whispered.

They stood in silence at a fork in the tunnel. Alfie realized that Robin was trying to decide which way to go. Murkle and Snitch's footsteps were very close now. "We've got to hide until they pass," he whispered, swaying dizzily. "We'll find her later." He gave a sharp tug on Robin's arm as he stood like a statue staring down the two passages. "Robin!"

"We heeeeear you," hissed a voice from the far side of the cavern.

"MADDIE, RUN!" Robin shouted at the top of his lungs as Alfie dragged him across the cavern.

"We seeeeee you," sneered the other voice.

Alfie dropped down and wriggled along the floor, followed by Robin. They wedged themselves between a crop of large stalagmites and the cave wall and lay still, hardly daring to breathe. Alfie's head throbbed with pain as he lay there in the dark. He twisted slightly to avoid something sharp that was digging into his ribs and suddenly realized what he was lying on. A mixture of horror and revulsion built inside him and he stifled a cry of disgust. They were surrounded by large animal bones—cows, sheep, even horse skulls. All of them had been picked completely clean. The dragon must live in these caves!

He stayed there for what seemed like forever. He couldn't hear anything other than his own blood pounding in his ears. Murkle and Snitch must have passed them by. He hoped that they hadn't taken the same path as Madeleine. He slowly lifted his head and opened his eyes.

"BOO!"

Alfie screamed as he felt Snitch's foul breath in his face. Robin grasped at his leg as Miss Murkle dragged him out of his hiding place by the ankles. Snitch grabbed Alfie by the hair and pulled him up until just the tips of his toes were touching the ground.

"You've been very busy, haven't you?" she hissed. "Sneaking and snooping."

"Peeking and prying," added Murkle.

Alfie struggled under her grip but Snitch's strength was incredible. The pain in his head was so intense he felt he would pass out.

"Okay! We'll come back with you," yelped Robin as Miss Murkle twisted his ear. "But we've got to find Madeleine first."

"Oh, we're not going back to the office," said Murkle breezily.

"But don't worry—we'll find your sister," said Snitch. "Now move!"

The sisters dragged the boys toward the branch of the forked passage and took the one that led downward. Alfie tried to brace himself against the rocky floor but was pulled along behind Snitch as though he weighed nothing at all.

"We know you stole my talisman because you want to open the seal under the castle," he yelled, sounding much braver than he felt as the pain blossomed in his shoulder and head.

"Oh, do you now?" sniggered Murkle, dragging Robin along beside her. "Well, aren't you the detective?"

"We know you're controlling the dragon too!" Alfie shouted, hoping to shock them into loosening their grip. At this the two sisters burst into peals of shrieking laughter.

"Yes," hissed Snitch. "And what are you going to do about it? Other than help us to wake the rest?"

Alfie couldn't believe what he was hearing. "What do you mean, wake the rest? You think there are more dragons somewhere?"

Snitch roared with laughter. "He doesn't know!" she screeched. "Nobody told him!"

"Told me what?" shouted Alfie as he pulled back uselessly against her grip.

"What you are living above," cackled Murkle as

Robin wheezed and struggled feebly against the arm she had wrapped around his neck. "What sleeps miles below your very own home . . ."

"Just tell me!"

Snitch pulled Alfie up by his shirt until they were nose to nose. "A dragon nest," she spat, her stinking breath making him retch as she dropped him to the floor. He stared up at his headmistresses as they shrieked with delight at the look on his face. Robin caught his eye and shook his head, obviously thinking the same as Alfie. They were stark staring mad. They had to get away. Snitch lurched forward as though she had read Alfie's mind, catching him in an iron grip and pulling him to his feet. He had no option but to stumble wretchedly forward as the sisters dragged them down into the depths of the caves. A smell of sulfur grew stronger as they went farther down. Alfie suddenly realized what was happening—the headmistresses were taking them straight to the dragon.

He dug his heels into the floor of the cave, fighting against Snitch's grip.

"What's the matter?" laughed Snitch. "Anyone would think you didn't want to meet the creature you seem so interested in." Before Alfie could answer back, something large brushed past his leg. He jerked in fright and heard a shriek from Murkle.

"Something bit me! *Argh*, it's got my hand! Get it off me!"

Snitch let go of Alfie's hair and began to shriek in pain; the creature must have bitten her too. He reached out and felt Robin's hands searching for him.

"Run!" he shouted. They scrambled up the slippery path, then raced back to the bone-strewn cavern, leaving the two screaming sisters behind them. Turning at the fork, they followed the path that led upward. The distant shrieking had stopped and the sisters were running through the passageways behind them. Alfie could hear a scratching noise like a dog running as whatever had attacked the headmistresses caught up with them. He expected to feel its jaws on his legs at any moment, but to his amazement it ran straight past, giving a series of short, high-pitched barks as though guiding them through the caves as it shot ahead.

"They're right behind us!" cried Robin as Murkle and Snitch furiously screeched and roared their way up the tunnel. Alfie could barely hear him—everything seemed to be fizzing in and out of focus. His legs started to wobble and he heard his cousin yell, "Come on! We're not going to make it out!" Alfie clutched at Robin's arm and tried to speak, but it was too late. He felt himself falling, taking Robin with him as the fuzziness filled his vision and faded to black.

CHAPTER SEVENTEEN

Into Mist

"Wake up, Alfie."

Robin was shaking him gently by the shoulder. Alfie struggled to pull his thoughts together and wondered why the cold, hard ground was suddenly soft and warm and smelled like sheep. He opened his eyes a crack and immediately shut them again as the sunlight sent a searing pain through his head. He sat up, cupped his hands around his eyes, and looked down into his lap as he got used to the brightness.

"Banged yourself up a bit, didn't you, lad?" said a gruff but jovial voice.

Touching his head gingerly, Alfie found that it was bound up with strips of cloth, as was his shoulder. His eyes watered slightly from the strong but not unpleasant herbal smell coming from the bandages.

"I've cleaned up the wound and applied some

liniment. Just cooked it up this morning—must have known you were coming."

Alfie blinked in the direction of the voice. The glare eased and he could make out a broad, bearded man sitting nearby, lighting a fire under a pot of water. He was wearing a coarse hempen shirt and trousers and a shaggy brown vest.

"Powerful stuff, that is," he said proudly. "Got the recipe from a good friend of mine. You'll heal up nicely."

Alfie thanked the strange man as he looked around groggily. He was sitting on a makeshift bed of bundles of wood and fleeces in a homey cave that opened out onto the forest. Robin was sitting beside him, knees drawn up to his chin as he hugged his legs.

"What happened?" he groaned. "Did you find Maddie?"

"No." Robin stared at his feet gloomily. "You've been in and out of consciousness for about half an hour. We should go to the hospital, but . . . I don't think they have them here. Not yet, anyway."

"What?" Alfie clambered to his feet and staggered to the cave mouth to gaze down at a familiar but different view of Hexbridge valley. Despite the splotches of color that danced across his vision, he could see just how different the landscape looked. The familiar patchwork of fields that surrounded Hexbridge were now shrouded in thick forest that stretched out across the valley, as far as he could see. Robin's words finally sank in as Alfie realized what this meant. It had happened again, like on the last day of the term. He had slipped back through time, but this time he had brought Robin with him.

"Everything went foggy when you passed out," said Robin, twisting the bottom of his sweater. "When it cleared we were still in the caves but Murkle and Snitch had gone. I couldn't move you so I went to get help. I met Bryn here; this is his cave. He carried you out of the tunnels and bandaged your head."

Bryn smiled as Alfie thanked him and politely admired his cave. "I use it for storage and to catch a bit of thinking time. You're lucky I was here today—the wife sent me to fetch some of the firewood you're sitting on."

"I wanted to go back and look for Maddie," said Robin, "but when I realized what had happened I knew it would be pointless." He looked down at the ground and said quietly, "She won't be there, will she?"

"I'm so sorry, Robin. I didn't mean to bring us here. It's just like the last time. I can't control it."

"If it hadn't happened they would have caught us," said Robin. "I don't know what they were going to do, but they weren't going to let us go. You saved us both, but I just wish I knew Madeleine was safe."

Alfie was grateful that Robin didn't blame him, but couldn't help being angry at himself. If he hadn't dragged them back through time, maybe they would have found Madeleine by now, or at least have a search party looking for her.

"Alfie, can you get us back home?" asked Robin.

"I'm not sure. Last time everything just faded and I was back. I didn't need to do anything. Maybe we're still here because I was unconscious so long?"

"Sounds as though you two need a bit of advice," said Bryn. "Just as well I sent word to a friend who always knows what to do. In fact, here he comes." He waved down the hill at a cloaked figure making his way up the trail. "Ho, Orin!" The figure below called out a distant greeting as he waved back.

"I don't believe it. That's Orin? Orin Hopcraft?" shouted Alfie, jumping back up despite the throbbing in his head. "Of course! We're in *his* time now. He'll know how to get us home!"

"Just like he got you and your kin home the night you were born," said Bryn.

Alfie turned to him in surprise. "You know about that?"

"Know about it? I was at the castle when your parents came through the mist. My wife helped deliver you. Orin said you'd be back one of these days. I can't say I expected you to turn up in my cave though."

"Nor did I!" laughed Orin Hopcraft, his gray eyes twinkling as he swept into the cave. His warm presence seemed to fill the entire space as he unclasped his long brown cloak and let it drop to the floor, revealing a dark green tunic over a loose long-sleeved shirt. The druid clapped his hands to Alfie's shoulders. "Alfie, my dear boy! How wonderful it is to see you again."

"Orin," Alfie stammered, struggling to think of something else to say as he took in the druid's neatly plaited beard and loosely tied, gray-streaked brown hair—just as his dad had described it. "Er, pleased to meet you. This is my cousin, Robin."

"Cousin Robin, a pleasure indeed!" said Orin. Robin stared up at the druid in awe as he shook his hand.

Orin sat down on his cloak and untied a small pouch

from his leather belt. "Bryn, could you make us some chamomile-and-valerian tea?" He handed over the pouch, and Bryn tipped the herbs it contained into the pot of water he had been boiling. Alfie breathed in the soothing scent that started to fill the cave. "Now, much as we have to talk about," said Orin, his voice soft and serious, "I would like to hear about the circumstances that brought you here."

Bryn poured four cups of the tea as Alfie recounted what had happened. Robin seemed very much in awe of Orin as Alfie told the druid all about Murkle and Snitch and the chase through the tunnels. Orin looked very worried by the fact that they'd had the talisman for several weeks, and he looked astounded to hear that they seemed to know of the seal in the cellars. When Alfie told him about the dragon they had seen and Murkle and Snitch's plan to use the talisman to wake the rest, Orin gripped his wooden cup so tightly his knuckles turned white.

"This dragon," said the druid, his voice dark. "Tell me, does it have two heads?"

"Yes!" said Alfie. "How did you know?"

"I have seen it myself," said Orin gravely. "When

Agrodonn came to force me to hand over the magic you now harbor."

"The allies he brought with him," cried Alfie, as he remembered Orin's letter, "the ones that torched the villagers' fields and slaughtered their livestock, they were dragons, weren't they?"

Orin nodded slowly.

"I don't believe this. Why didn't you tell me?"

"I think my letter contained enough information that would be hard for you to take in. I didn't want to add dragons to the list, not when I thought that this one had suffered the same fate as its brother."

"Then tell me *now*," said Alfie, wincing at a fresh stab of pain in his temple. "Murkle and Snitch said there's a dragon's nest under the castle. That's what they're after. Is it true?"

The druid nodded to Bryn to pour some more tea. He took a deep draft from his cup and sighed. "It is true. The age of dragons is long gone, and now they sleep in forgotten places deep within the earth. Hexbridge is above the last gateway to these places. Agrodonn knew this. He traveled down into the earth for many days until he found two small dragons. He used a control magic to bend them to his will, and when I refused to hand over my creation magic, he ordered them to burn the fields. As they snatched up and devoured cows and sheep, he told me that the people would be next. That is why I had no choice but to use the magic I gave you against him. When it fed on his power, he could no longer control the dragons and they swooped away over the hills.

"When I used my freshly fed magic to create the castle, I chose to do so over the gateway Agrodonn had opened, creating a great seal over it that only the talisman can open. I didn't need to hunt down the dragons that he had awoken—a knight in Lambton killed one soon after, and I had heard that your dragon had suffered a similar fate. But I was wrong."

Orin looked at Alfie, his soft gray eyes betraying the great concern he felt.

Alfie gazed back, his excitement at meeting the druid melting against a little flame that flickered inside him. "So they aren't totally crazy, then. As well as being your hiding place for a magic that I didn't even have a choice in taking, the castle, *my home*, is the only thing between the world and a load of sleeping dragons?"

Alfie stared at the druid, wondering if the castle was really worth all of that. He thought about asking Orin to take back the magic along with the castle and the talisman, if that was even possible—but would it make him a coward? He hadn't asked for any of this, and now Madeleine was lost and alone while he was sitting in the past drinking tea.

"I was wrong to keep it from you," said Orin. "I knew you would be quite safe as long as the seal remained intact. I hadn't counted on anyone in your day and age knowing of its existence." He leaned forward earnestly and placed his hand on Alfie's shoulder. "I made a mistake. Can you forgive me?"

Alfie shrugged one of his shoulders as he stared at the floor. The castle had helped him escape his old life and had brought him closer to his dad, but he was starting to wonder what the true cost of that would be. Finally, he nodded.

"Thank you, Alfie." Orin smiled.

"But you can't keep anything that big from me ever again—and I need your help. What can I do to stop them?"

"I don't know what kind of villains these teachers of yours are," said Orin, "but it takes a strong will to control a dragon. At least they don't seem to be aware of the magic you hold. I will send a note to Caspian to provide you with some extra protection until he can do something about the creature."

"You know Caspian?" asked Alfie, surprised to hear the name on the druid's lips. "Can he time travel too?"

"He has his own ways of conducting business," said Orin. "But that one is old—older than you would ever imagine. Now, until the dragon has been dealt with, don't provoke these teachers of yours, and never let them catch you on your own."

"I wouldn't worry about that," Robin piped up angrily. "They'll be locked up as soon as we tell our parents what happened."

"Perhaps," said Orin, "but the slipperiest eels are the most difficult to catch. I may have something that will help you. Alfie, I will prepare what you need and send instructions through Caspian. It will help you to alert others as to what these sisters are up to. Now come, we'll help you down the hill before you travel home."

Robin started to protest, but Orin placed his hands on his shoulders and said softly, "I know you need to find your sister, but you should not look for her alone. You need to get help before going back into the caves."

"Well, can you send us back to before they chased us?" asked Robin. "Then we can send ourselves help."

"I'm sorry. The clock keeps ticking wherever you are—when you return home, the time you have spent here will have elapsed there too."

"Then what are we waiting for?" Robin rushed impatiently ahead down the narrow forest trail as Alfie stumbled along behind, supported by Bryn and Orin.

"Tell me, Alfie," said Orin. "Were you in peril at any time when you weren't wearing the talisman?"

Alfie started to shake his head but Robin had bounced back to speed them along and piped up. "Of course you were. What about the fire in the school hall? You and Jimmy could have been burned to a crisp!"

"And during this fire, did anything unusual happen at the height of danger?"

Alfie told the druid about the pain and jolts he had felt as he tried to rescue his friend.

"Because you have lived with the magic since you were a baby, you can control it better than anyone else ever could," said Orin. "It is ancient and powerful and will protect its bearer in order to protect itself. However, as you are untrained in magic, it could seriously hurt you even when trying to defend you.

"For now, the talisman helps control and focus the raw energy—it stops it from shining like a beacon to anyone searching for it. You must wear it always and keep it hidden. As you get older the magic will become more active. You must learn to control the part of it that wants to be free to feed and create. I will teach you this when your training begins. You are more than its guardian—you are its prison."

They walked in silence for the rest of the journey. Alfie knew now that the castle had come at a great price after all. He could see in the druid's eyes the terrible guilt he felt for burdening him with the magic and all that it entailed.

The trees thinned out toward the bottom of the hill. Bryn's expression was a mixture of pride and embarrassment as the boys thanked him for his help.

"Always happy to help friends of Orin. Make sure you come and see me the next time you visit. The wife would love to see you again. She'll feed you till you're fed up." Alfie smiled weakly as Bryn slapped him on the back and strode off whistling loudly, his bale of firewood under one arm.

As they crossed a narrow dirt track, Robin spotted a milestone and let out a yell. "I know this stone! It's right near the entrance to our farm . . . it's still there in—" Robin never finished his sentence as he disappeared with an almost audible pop.

Alfie stared at the empty space where Robin had stood a second before as he half toppled, half sat down on the grass.

"It looks as though your cousin has found his own way home," smiled Orin as he crouched down next to Alfie. "This will be a little harder for you. Both times are equally your home."

"Will I be able to visit you again?" asked Alfie, his aching head reeling with all of the many questions he wanted to ask the druid.

"Eventually," said Orin. "I hope that one day you will learn to master traveling between our two times. When that happens, your training will begin."

"Training?" said Alfie. "You said something about that in your letter. You mean I could become a druid, like you?"

"I can teach you as little or as much as you like to know of our ways and earth magics," said Orin. "But only if you wish it."

Alfie thought of all that he might learn from Orin— knowledge that was likely long lost in his own time. "I'd like that very much."

Orin smiled. "Well then, until we meet again. Now, to help you join young Robin. Close your eyes. Breathe deeply as you relax and think about your own time."

Alfie closed his eyes and followed the druid's instructions, concentrating his mind on modern-day Hexbridge.

"Tell me, do you feel a pulling sensation in the center of your chest?"

Alfie gradually became aware of the feeling the druid described. "Yes. It's very faint . . . it feels like something is dragging me toward it."

"Focus on your home and the universe will try to pull you back there. All you have to do is let it."

Alfie focused on the feeling of belonging he felt in Hexbridge. He tried to let all other thoughts drift away. The sensation began to spread through his body.

"Good, good," said Orin's voice, fainter now. "Keep letting yourself be pulled out of time."

The pain in Alfie's head was making it difficult to maintain concentration. He was about to tell Orin when the words were whisked from his mouth as he was dragged across six hundred years in a second. Opening his eyes, he found himself sitting in the lane that led up to the Merryweather farm. He could see Robin in the distance. "Robin!" he called, reeling as he staggered to his feet. His cousin raced back down the lane and hooked his arm under Alfie's shoulder.

"Come on, Alfie, we've got to tell everyone what

happened." Alfie was surprised at his cousin's strength; he felt like the slow lumbering partner in a three-legged race as they stumbled toward the farm.

As they came in sight of the farmhouse, he spotted Uncle Herb, Aunt Grace, and Granny getting into the truck. A sad little face was looking out of one of the back windows, chin resting forlornly on the sill.

"Maddie!" shouted Robin, practically dropping Alfie as he dashed toward the truck. Alfie hurried after him as everyone leapt out and ran toward them. Madeleine reached them first. She hugged them both tightly and Alfie saw that her dirty face was streaked with tears. Her knees were grazed and her sweater was torn from running down the hill and through the briars.

"I was so scared," she sobbed. "I waited for you for ages. I thought they'd taken you down into the caves and we'd never find you."

"Maddie, what happened to you?" asked Alfie.

"You shouldn't have run ahead," said Robin before she could answer. "I told you not to. You just panicked and ran off. You could have been lost forever!"

"I thought I *was* lost!" said Madeleine excitedly, forgetting her tears. "But then a fox appeared—it kept stopping and barking—it wanted me to follow it, I could tell. Can you believe it? A fox! It ran back into the caves after leading me out. Did you see it? I'm sure it was the one we sometimes see in the village."

"Well, if it's the same one that took two chickens last week, then it's welcome to them," said Uncle Herb.

Alfie's head was starting to throb again when he saw his dad's car bouncing down the lane.

"Alfie, what happened?" his dad called, scrambling out of the car and hugging him tightly. "Maddie said you'd been kidnapped."

"Murkle and Snitch," gulped Alfie, blinking hard as everything began to look a little blurry. "They stole my talisman. They caught us when we took it back and tried to drag us off into the caves."

"Slow down," said his dad. "What do you mean they tried to drag you into the caves? Look at your head! Did they do this to you?"

"It happened while they were chasing us." Alfie felt sick with effort as he tried to focus on his dad. "I know this sounds crazy, but the missing animals—they're being taken by a dragon! Murkle and Snitch are controlling it and they want to wake the rest."

"He's telling the truth!" said Robin as everyone stared

at Alfie in astonishment. "We've all seen it. It inciner-ated Mrs. Emmett."

"Murkle and Snitch are totally crazy," added Madeleine. "We've got to do something!"

"And we will," said Granny firmly, recovering her composure before everyone else. "I want to hear all about this, but first things first." She lifted Alfie's chin and stared into his eyes as she pushed up one of his eyelids with her thumb. "You, my dear, are going to the hospital."

Several hours later, Alfie was sitting propped up in a hospital bed waiting impatiently for his dad. He tried reading to pass the time, but all he had been given was a booklet on healthy eating and a pile of torn picture books that had been scribbled on. A doctor had told him that he had a concussion and would need to stay under obser-vation for a while. She had instructed the nurses to check on him every half hour. This was beginning to annoy Alfie. Every time they popped in he thought it was his dad arriving.

He lay back and watched the minute hand on the ward

clock click to half past seven. The whole Merryweather clan had gone to the school with his dad and the police to confront the headmistresses. Inspector Wainwright had taken their story very seriously and had called up most of Hexbridge's small police force to accompany them to the school. That was several hours ago. Alfie wondered what was keeping them. He was dying to know exactly what Murkle and Snitch's faces had looked like as they were led away in handcuffs.

One of the nurses popped in to test Alfie's reflexes with a little rubber hammer when he heard voices coming down the corridor. His cousins bounced into the ward, closely followed by his dad.

"We thought you'd be bored so I brought you some books," said Robin, replacing the tatty picture books with an encyclopedia, a survival handbook, and a collection of adventure stories.

"I got you some tongue twizzlers and sherbet fizz-bombs from Gertie Entwhistle's," said Madeleine, plonking a white paper bag on top of the books.

"How's the noggin?" asked his dad as he sat down next to the bed and handed Alfie a flask. "Chicken soup," he said with a smile. "Granny said she'll bring you another batch when she comes to visit tomorrow."

Alfie was confused. He thought that everyone would have been bursting to get back and tell him what happened at the school, but they had stopped off at the sweetshop and even found time to wait for Granny to make soup.

"Well?" he asked expectantly.

"Well what?" asked his dad.

"What happened at the school? You've been ages. I thought you'd have come straight back to tell me all about it."

"You mean the accident?" asked Robin, confused.

"No, not my accident!" yelled Alfie in frustration, which made the nurse pop his head around the curtains of the next bed to shush him. "What happened when the police arrested Murkle and Snitch? Did they try to run away?"

Everyone went quiet. Robin and Madeleine glanced at each other uneasily. His dad looked concerned and squeezed his hand. "Why on earth would anyone arrest your teachers? Don't you remember what happened today?"

"Of course I remember." Alfie looked around as though this was a bad joke, but nobody laughed. "We got my talisman back from Murkle and Snitch's office.

They chased us through the secret passage from their office into the caves in the hills. Murkle and Snitch caught me and Robin. I hit my head as we were running from them."

He looked at the three serious faces around the bed and realized that they weren't just pretending not to know what he was talking about—they really didn't have a clue.

"Alfie," said Robin in a worried voice, "we were climbing one of the trees behind the school at lunchtime, and you fell and hit your head on the way down. Don't you remember? Murkle and Snitch were really good about it, even though we were off the school grounds. They drove us back to the castle. You were so dizzy you hardly knew what was going on. We were all really worried."

"We brought you straight here after they dropped you off," added his dad. "The nurses were very impressed with how well they fixed up your head."

Alfie listened to this with mounting confusion. What was going on?

"They didn't bandage my head! That was Bryn, the man who helped Robin carry me out of the cave before we traveled back from the past." His dad gave his hand another concerned squeeze. Alfie thought back over the afternoon's events. They were so clear in his mind.

The nurse appeared again and started to usher everyone out of the room so that Alfie could sleep. As they were leaving, a few things struck Alfie as odd.

"Wait!" he called after his cousins. "I've never seen Murkle and Snitch drive before. What type of car was it?"

"Um, I can't remember," said the usually observant Robin.

Hah! thought Alfie as his cousin's face screwed up in thought. "Come on, describe it, what color was it? What were the seats like? Was it big, small, old, new? Who was driving?"

"I can't remember who drove," said Madeleine. "I think the car was . . . maybe green?" She looked to Robin, who shrugged and then nodded in agreement.

"Well, which tree did I fall out of?" said Alfie quickly. "All the trees behind the school are pines; you can't climb them."

Robin and Madeleine started to look confused and scared as Alfie fired question after question at them.

"Who went to get Murkle and Snitch after I fell out of the tree? How long was I unconscious? Where did you go after you left me here? Tell me the *details*!"

"That's enough, Alfie," said his dad firmly. "I know this is frightening for you, but you need to calm down now or you'll make yourself worse." He gently ruffled Alfie's hair. "Don't think about it too hard tonight. Just sleep. You'll feel better after some rest."

After everyone said their good-byes and left the ward, Alfie felt worse than ever. He settled down into the narrow hospital bed as the nurse poured him a glass of water and pulled the curtains closed.

"Nurse," he asked just before he disappeared, "when we arrived at the hospital, do you remember what we told you about my accident?"

"I do," said the nurse, his eyes glazing over slightly. "You were climbing a tree behind the school and you fell and knocked your head. Miss Snitch filled me in on the details when she came by about an hour ago. She didn't want to disturb you—just asked how you are. Wasn't that nice?"

He closed the curtains and Alfie lay in the darkness struggling to think through the throbbing pain in his head. It was then that he remembered the talisman. He clapped his hand to his chest and felt it safely fastened around his neck under the hospital gown. They really had been into Murkle and Snitch's office.

His head reeled as he realized that if what he remembered was the truth, Murkle and Snitch had somehow twisted the memories of all of his family, as well as the police. The realization was so frightening that he almost wished he had been wrong after all. Lying cold and afraid under the thin hospital blankets, Alfie felt more alone than ever before.

CHAPTER EIGHTEEN

An Unexpected Ally

Alfie spent most of the next week in bed glaring up at the animals carved into the wooden canopy above his bed. He was thoroughly miserable. Madeleine and Robin visited every day with news of the dress rehearsals for the play. Each time, Alfie interrogated them about the accident and tried to remind them about the chase through the tunnels, but they just looked at him pityingly. His entire family suddenly thought that Murkle and Snitch were wonderful human beings—it was all Alfie could do not to scream. Murkle and Snitch were tearing everything away from him, and with no one to talk to, he couldn't figure out what to do about it.

His only consolation was that he was away from school for the time being, and the dragon seemed unable to penetrate the castle's grounds. He had a feeling it was due to the castle being built by magic. Now he just needed to stop Murkle and Snitch from getting inside.

He wondered if there was a way he could withdraw his offer of hosting the school play without everyone at school hating him forever. If only his dad would stop checking on him every ten minutes, he might be able to think straight.

By the end of the week, he was so desperate for something to do that he decided to clean his room. Sorting through the mounds of clothes, comics, and schoolbooks, he wondered if his dad's room looked just as bad—he imagined it was probably worse. A loud knock on the door made him jump and bang his head as he was scrabbling around under the bed to retrieve a last dirty sock.

"Telephone call," called Ashford as Alfie crawled out, wiping the balls of dust from his jeans. He noticed the butler glance at the talisman around his neck, then quickly look away. Alfie tucked it into his T-shirt and glared at Ashford. He didn't know who he could trust anymore. He had started locking his door at night and tried to avoid his dad and the butler as much as possible.

"Caspian Bone wishes to speak with you," said Ashford, looking slightly wounded by Alfie's reaction. Alfie hurried past him and down the stairs. He hadn't spoken to Caspian since moving day. What could he want?

"Good afternoon," said the lawyer almost as soon as the receiver touched Alfie's ear. "I hope that this call finds you convalesced?"

Alfie didn't bother asking how Caspian knew about his accident and let him continue uninterrupted.

"Orin Hopcraft left a message to be delivered to you on this date. He believed that you would be sufficiently recovered from your ordeal by now and wished for you to visit his study on this night."

In all the anger and loneliness he had felt since his family had been hypnotized by Murkle and Snitch, Alfie had completely forgotten that Orin had promised to send him help.

"He asked that you look inside the wooden box on his desk," said Caspian. "The key will come to you."

"How did he give you the message?" Alfie burst out before he could stop himself.

"May I remind you that Muninn and Bone is a VERY long-established firm—1086, to be precise," replied Caspian. "We save a great many messages, documents, and items to pass on when the time is right, never before. This is one such message. Now, I believe you may have noticed our sentinels posted around the castle?"

Alfie looked out through one of the windows. He hadn't seen anyone around. Then he noticed the unusual number of ravens outside: at least two on every wall and several circling overhead.

"I see them, but why are they here?" asked Alfie.

"The Great Druid wished us to look out for you at this time."

"So you know about Murkle and Snitch?" said Alfie. "Can you help me to . . ."

"I do not need to know the details," said Caspian. "I have passed on Orin's message and bid you good day."

Alfie stared at the receiver in surprise as the line clicked and the dial tone hummed through the earpiece. He had a good mind to call Caspian straight back and shout until he listened, but settled for kicking the umbrella stand, which unfortunately turned out to be made of cast iron.

Orin hadn't specified a time, so Alfie waited until his dad was in bed and unlikely to check on him. Just after midnight, he grabbed a torch from his wall and scurried along the corridor to the library.

Lighting the candles in Orin's study, he sat down at the druid's desk and reached for the wooden box that sat in the center, as if placed there just for him. There was a small keyhole on the front, but he didn't have the key. Caspian had said it would come to him. Was that some form of riddle, or had he forgotten to send it? As he turned the box over in his hands, there were footsteps from the passage that led into the study. Someone was coming through and it didn't sound like his dad.

"Who's there?" he croaked fearfully as a tall figure slipped into the room. The candlelight glinted off a sharp, curved blade in the hand of the shadowy figure.

"What do you want?" Alfie demanded, sounding braver than he felt. He lifted the box over his head, ready to use it as a weapon.

"I've brought something for you," said a soft, familiar voice. Ashford stepped out of the shadows. "Now maybe you should put that down before you break whatever is inside."

Alfie backed away, the box still held high. "Why have you got a knife?" Alfie could barely keep the wobble out of his voice as he found himself backed up against the shelves with nowhere else to go.

"This?" said Ashford, looking down at the blade in his hand. "I brought this for you." He swung his arm out toward Alfie, who leapt aside to dodge the blade, holding the box to his chest as a shield between himself and the butler.

Ashford froze, hand held out in front of him, horror written all over his face. Alfie looked down. The butler was offering him the knife, handle first. Was this some kind of trick? His fingers shook as he reached out to take it. Ashford seemed mortified by his reaction.

"You thought I was going to hurt you?" he exclaimed. "I'm so sorry. It's a ceremonial sickle—part of a family heirloom. I believe you'll need it in order to follow the instructions in that box."

Alfie stared at the butler.

"Caspian passed this on to me in a message from Orin." Ashford held out a small silver key. "I was to bring it here at this time so that you would know to trust me. I hope I haven't jeopardized that trust?"

"How could Orin possibly know you?" asked Alfie, sinking into Orin's armchair. "Who are you really?"

"Your faithful butler," said Ashford, with absolute sincerity. "Now, let's get this box open. I have been asked to help you with its contents."

Inside the box was what looked like a shopping list of strange items, packets of dried roots, small colored crystals, and a letter. Alfie opened it and read aloud:

Dear Alfie,

Despite the terrible circumstances of our meet-ing, it was a pleasure to finally speak to you in person. It is clear that the two women you are facing must be revealed for their true selves and stopped before they can attempt to carry out their plans. I have asked Caspian to pro-vide you with some protection, but for the sake of the continued containment of the magic you guard, you must learn to defend yourself against such enemies.

I am sending this spell of revelation to help you. I am also leaving some of the items you will need for this potion. The rest would not survive the passage of time, which is why I have asked Muninn and Bone to arrange for someone to help you. If it is the soul I have requested, he will be able to perform the incantation on the back of this letter, instruct you in the potions preparation, and find the remaining ingredients. However, I must warn you not to ask him more than he can tell you. He must remain silent on his past: to speak of it would jeopardize his very existence.

Your friend always,
Orin Hopcraft

Alfie flipped the letter over to reveal a string of runes and stared up at Ashford in amazement. "But, how . . . ?"

The butler pretended to twist a key between his lips as he took the list from the box. "Let's see: yarrow, black salt, agrimony, mandrake root, dragon's blood . . ."

"Dragon's blood?" gasped Alfie. "How are we going to get *that*?"

"It's a resin, not real blood," said Ashford. "I might even have some handy. Everything else on this list is easy enough. I can have it all by tomorrow night. You can get this one."

"Mistletoe?" read Alfie.

"There's some growing on the oak in the courtyard. It must be cut with a silver sickle under the moonlight, so use the one I've given you to collect some before we meet here at midnight tomorrow. Cut a little extra if you like." He smiled. "Isn't Miss Siu visiting again for Christmas?"

Alfie glared as Ashford smiled innocently back at him.

Alfie felt ten times better the next day. Now there was at least one person in the world he could talk to. He read Orin's letter again, wondering if Ashford would really be able to find all of the strange ingredients so quickly. The ravens were still stationed around the castle. He waved at them every time he passed a window, but was hardly surprised when they ignored him completely.

At eleven o'clock, he got dressed and padded down to the courtyard. Standing on the bench around the oak, he cut down a piece of mistletoe and felt himself blushing furiously as he thought of Amy. Ashford obviously didn't understand that a girl and a boy could just be friends without any of that . . . that . . . stuff!

Ashford joined him in Orin's study at midnight and set him to work with the pestle and mortar. Alfie used the opportunity to release some of the anger and frustration he had felt over the last week as he pounded the colored crystals and tree resins into powder. While he worked, Ashford chopped the herbs and crushed the juice out of the berries with one of his silver blades.

"If this works on Murkle and Snitch," said Alfie, mashing at the powder in the mortar as though it was his teachers' heads, "will everyone get their memories back?"

"Without knowing exactly what they did, I can't be sure," said Ashford, tipping the powder, herbs, and juice into a small purple bottle of liquid and carrying it over to the window. "It reveals deep, dangerous secrets as well as someone's true nature. If there are any enchantments surrounding them, it is likely that they will all be undone and then we can stop them." Alfie hoped that this included the weird hypnosis they had worked on everyone.

Sitting on the sill was a bowl of water lined with oak leaves and colored crystals shining gently in the moonlight. Ashford carefully added some of the water to the bottle, then began to read the runic incantation on the back of Orin's letter. Alfie listened to the strange language flowing so easily from Ashford's lips and wondered where he had learned it. Finishing the incantation, the butler corked the bottle and passed it to Alfie. "Shake it," he ordered. "Imagine it stripping away all of the secrets and lies from your Murkle and Snitch."

Alfie took the bottle and shook until his arms hurt, picturing everyone seeing the two women revealed for their terrible selves. Finally, when his arms felt like jelly, he held the bottle up to the window. Against the bright white moon he could see little motes of light floating gently behind the purple glass—it was like a tiny universe filled with stars.

"So I just throw it over Murkle and Snitch and they'll admit what they did and what they're planning to do? Everyone will be able to see how crazy they really are?"

"It will have a mild effect if splashed on the skin. In order to work its full magic, they will need to drink a few drops." His voice took on a very serious tone as he added, "They obviously have strong abilities of their own and won't be happy at the results of this potion. For your own safety, make sure that as many people as possible are present to help you if needed."

Alfie smiled grimly. The danger was worth it if it meant getting his headmistresses out of his life and having his family back to normal.

"I see you got the talisman back," said Ashford as Alfie turned to leave.

"You know about it?" asked Alfie. "Murkle and Snitch stole it."

Ashford nodded. "Not the first time it has been stolen. The last thief was the one who gave it to Orin Hopcraft."

"Who was that?" asked Alfie, but he need not have asked—he could see the answer written on Ashford's face.

"Perhaps I'll be able to tell you about it, some day." He smiled.

Back in his room, Alfie hid the bottle away in one of the secret compartments in his bed. Lying in the dark, waiting for sleep to arrive, he tried to fathom how he was going to get Murkle and Snitch to drink the potion. Nestling into his pillow, he consoled himself with one thought—at least he knew where he was going to do it. The play would go ahead!

CHAPTER NINETEEN

Curtain Up

Alfie stood in the minstrels' gallery with Madeleine and Robin, gazing down at the Great Hall in awe. The twins had finally started to relax around him again since he had stopped talking about Murkle and Snitch, but it was horrible to feel as though he couldn't trust his cousins while they were under the headmistresses' influence. Alfie's insides were tying themselves in knots. It was the morning of the school play—the day Murkle and Snitch would be exposed and stopped before they could carry out their crazy plan to open the trapdoor and bring dragons back into the world. Classes had been canceled so that everyone could rehearse at the castle. Ashford had just reopened the hall after declaring it off-limits for two days.

The transformation of the Great Hall was unbelievable. The long dining table had disappeared and row upon row of ornate gold-colored chairs faced a grand stage now reaching from wall to wall at the far end of the room. A thick velvet curtain of the darkest blue hung from the ceiling, screening the performance area. In the already grand Great Hall the whole setup looked even more impressive than a real theater.

The two large brass spotlights attached to the rail suddenly flared into life, creating a circle of light on the center of the curtain, from behind which Alfie could hear a distant trumpet fanfare building in volume. The curtains suddenly swooshed aside to reveal Ashford in the center of the stage. The fanfare he was playing filled the hall. He ended it with a flourish and bowed to the assembled chairs.

"Just testing the acoustics," he called as the twins applauded loudly. "I'm also on lights and curtain duty today." He gestured proudly at the stage around him. "Well? What do you think of your performance arena?"

Alfie thought the stage looked amazing. The cutout trees and houses that had filled the art rooms had been positioned carefully in order of size to give the impression of depth. It was perfect.

"I take your silence as the highest of accolades," announced the butler, aiming a small device at the spotlights and switching them both off with one click.

"Who helped him to do all of this?" asked Madeleine.

Alfie shook his head as he watched Ashford cheerfully straightening chairs and moving suits of armor to stand at each side of the stage like proud sentries. He had shared his plans with the butler, who had promised to be on hand to help. He felt comforted by that promise. Whoever Ashford was, Alfie was glad he was on his side.

The day rolled on, and all of the teachers and pupils involved in the play began arriving at the castle. The stage had been built in front of the Abernathy Room, which had been converted into a dressing room that could be accessed from the wings of the stage. Some of the older kids had claimed half of the room for hair and makeup and were currently busy applying beards, wrinkles, and scars to the boys playing the parts of older men. Alfie noticed Madeleine hanging around looking for an opportunity to steal some hairy rubber warts.

Mr. Ramdhay had gotten the school band set up in the minstrels' gallery. Alfie couldn't believe the noise as the hall filled with a chorus of instruments being tuned and drums and cymbals being bashed and clashed.

All around him, the actors were practicing fighting with cardboard swords—Miss Reynard had drawn the line at using real swords from the castle.

After his stage makeup had been applied, Alfie changed into his squire outfit and tucked the purple bottle of potion into the leather pouch on his belt. Most of his role would be performed in the first half of the play, so he had offered to help Gertie Entwhistle serve refreshments during the intermission. When Murkle and Snitch came over for a drink, he would be the one to serve them. He had perfected hiding the bottle in the palm of his hand so that he could pour the liquid into their cups unnoticed.

Emerging from the narrow passage that led from backstage to the bustling hall, Alfie saw that the headmistresses had arrived. He ducked back behind the curtain, both relieved and terrified to see them. If they were planning on stealing the talisman from him again, they didn't stand a chance. He was ready for them. He gritted his teeth as Granny took them a tray of tea and cake. He couldn't wait to show everyone the truth.

Seven o'clock drew closer and Alfie began to feel very nervous. All performers were herded backstage as the hall started to fill up. He kept checking that the purple bottle was still in his pouch as he helped Cormac Feeney to strap on his breastplate. He hoped that by exposing the sisters in a hall full of people they could be stopped without any real danger—but if they could threaten children and change people's memories, who knew what else they were capable of?

A hush fell over the busy dressing room as Miss Reynard clapped her hands. "Okay, actors and actresses, the curtain goes up in three minutes! Line up in the order we rehearsed. Those entering from stage left, follow Mrs. Salvador—stage right, follow me."

The room was filled with commotion as everyone rushed to their correct places.

"Quietly!" hushed Miss Reynard, straightening Merlin's hat and rearranging the line. As the cast filed up the stairs to wait silently in the stage wings, Alfie wondered if Orin had ever worn a pointy hat.

The muffled voices from the hall suddenly went silent as the school band struck up the opening score. In the darkness of the wings, Alfie could feel the tension of dozens of nervous performers around him. His own heart pounded against his chest. He had been so preoccupied with confronting Murkle and Snitch that he had forgotten to be nervous about acting in front of a hall full of people. At this moment he wasn't sure which thought scared him the most.

The music reached its climax, then faded into the soft violin solo that marked the start of the play. The curtain went up as Mr. Ramdhay put on his most impressive voice and began narrating, taking the audience back in time to an England of noble heroes, brave knights, and dastardly foes—of wizardry, superstition, and a land in need of a king. Hearing their cue, the cast filed out onto the stage and began to sing about the mysterious sword in the stone.

The first song ended and the singers stepped back to become an audience to the tournament taking place center stage. The knights threw themselves into their roles, performing the graceful fight choreography Mr. Ramdhay had spent hours teaching them. Alfie squinted to see past the glare of the spotlights into the audience as he watched the tournament with his fellow squires. To the right of the front row he could just make out the smiling faces of his dad, aunt, uncle, and granny. At first he thought that there was an empty chair in the middle of the group, but two glowing green orbs revealed that Galileo had acquired a front row seat of his own.

"Squire, fetch me a weapon that I may show these

lumbering clods the grace with which a real knight wields a sword!"

Alfie snapped back into character and delivered his one line with a nod. "At once, Sir Kay." He did his best to look as if he was searching for a sword as the knights continued sparring. The band began to play softly as he approached the sword in the stone at the side of the stage. The music grew in volume and the audience cheered as he pulled out the sword in slow motion and held it aloft. Alfie heard Ashford play the trumpet fanfare he had been practicing as he was crowned king in the center of the stage.

Smoke machines at the sides of the stage spewed out a swirling mist, screening the cast from view. The villagers filed quickly offstage as stagehands rolled away the houses and replaced them with trees and rocks. The knights lined up facing the front of the stage, screened from the audience by the smoke. Cormac took the center spot and Alfie handed him the crown before hurrying from the stage just as Mr. Ramdhay announced, "Scotland, ten years hence."

With a roar, the knights charged through the smoke toward the audience, led by the older King Arthur. Reaching the edge of the stage, they turned sharply and began to fight the screaming Saxons charging out from the wings. Thunder effects rumbled over the war cries as flashing stage lights created lightning.

"This is brilliant!" whispered Jimmy as they stood in the wings behind a large fan that was making the mist swirl around the battlefield. Alfie didn't reply. He could see Murkle and Snitch sitting smirking in the front row. He knew they wouldn't head to the cellars yet. Not while he had the key. He was sure they were going to slip away in the commotion after the play ended, hiding in the castle until everyone else had gone. Well, they wouldn't have the chance. He was ready for them.

"Back to the dressing room, boys," Mrs. Salvador whispered loudly as she led the Saxon reinforcements into the wings behind them. "Hurry-hurry. No hanging about during the performance."

As Jimmy opened the dressing-room door, Alfie headed for the passage along the side of the stage.

"Hey, where are you going?"

"Just making sure Mrs. Entwhistle can find everything she needs. Catch you at the intermission."

Alfie slipped through the kitchens to help Gertie set up the refreshments table in the entrance hall. He was ready to take on Murkle and Snitch. At intermission, he clasped the little bottle in the palm of his hand and handed out glasses of juice to the performers and audience, all the time looking out for the headmistresses. He hoped that they would ask for juice, otherwise he'd have to find a way to slip it into the mulled wine Gertie was serving to the adults.

"Wonderful performances, my little thespians," said Granny as she swept up to the table with Madeleine and Robin.

"I didn't realize you were so talented," said his dad as he joined them. "You were the best actor up there!"

"Dad!" hissed Alfie, checking to make sure none of his school friends had heard. "I only said four words."

"Well, you said them with conviction," said his dad proudly.

"Have either of you seen Murkle and Snitch?" Alfie asked the twins as his dad and Granny headed back to their seats.

"No, I haven't seen *Miss* Murkle or *Miss* Snitch since the intermission started," said Madeleine, placing extra emphasis on their titles.

"Why are you looking for them?" asked Robin.

The twins were wearing the same slightly glazed and guarded expression Alfie had noticed on their faces whenever he had mentioned the headmistresses since the afternoon in the tunnels.

"I just realized that I haven't thanked them for looking after me yet," said Alfie, trying as hard as he possibly could to sound genuine. "They're my heroes." He thought he might have overdone it a bit, but the twins' faces immediately broke into smiles.

"Oh, how nice," said Madeleine.

"I'm sure they'd appreciate that," said Robin. "If we see them we'll tell them to find you."

"No need," said Alfie quickly. "I've got a gift for them and I want it to be a surprise." He didn't like lying to his cousins, but he didn't want Murkle and Snitch to suspect a thing.

The audience took their seats and the band played the opening music to the second act. Alfie gazed despairingly at the potion in this hand—he had missed his chance. The headmistresses would have to return to the Great Hall before the end of the performance to make a speech, but how could he possibly get them to drink the potion in front of everyone? Then it hit him—maybe they didn't have to drink the potion the usual way. He rushed to the kitchen, opened the stopper, and carefully poured the contents of the purple bottle into two special containers he took from the kitchen drawer. When they were full he tucked them safely into the back of his belt.

"Shouldn't you be backstage with the others?" asked Gertie, rolling a cart full of plastic cups and dirty wineglasses into the kitchen.

"Just on my way now," said Alfie. He began to follow her out of the kitchen but something caught his eye. The door to the undercroft was ajar. Murkle and Snitch must be down there already. But why? They didn't have the key. Had they figured out a way of getting through without it? He opened the door and paused at the top of the stairs. This wasn't what he had planned, but he had to know what they were doing down there. Taking a deep breath, he grabbed his dad's heavy rubber flashlight from the shelf by the door and rushed down the steps.

CHAPTER TWENTY

The Final Act

Alfie raced through the cellars. He hadn't brought the keys, but he didn't need them—the heavy reinforced door that led to the lower levels was wide open. His shoes echoed loudly as he started down the stone steps, so he took them off and continued the descent barefoot and silent. Even the dimmest setting on the flashlight seemed too bright, so he removed the woolen neck cloth from his costume and used it to cover the beam, leaving just enough light to see where he was going.

Tiptoeing through the larger chambers, he noticed a flickering orange light coming from the far corner where he had found the huge seal. He switched off the flashlight and was about to creep toward it when a hand clamped over his mouth and he felt himself being pulled backward.

"It's me, don't make a sound," Ashford whispered, dragging Alfie behind one of the stone columns. "Don't go any closer. You made quite a racket running through the upper cellars; they may know you're down here."

"What are they doing?" mouthed Alfie as silently as possible as the light intensified. He ducked back behind the pillar as a wave of heat stung his eyes.

"Trying to burn the trapdoor open," Ashford whispered back. "I don't know what they're using, but it won't work. That seal is impenetrable. It would be easier to dig through the rock around it with a plastic spoon."

Alfie was surprised Ashford even knew about the seal. The light died away and a growl of frustration echoed through the cellars. He wondered how the sisters could stand the intense heat.

"It's no use," called Snitch's voice. "We won't get through like this. We need the key."

"Come on," whispered Ashford. "They can't open it—not unless they find you down here."

"Sister?" called Snitch, as Alfie and Ashford crept toward the steps. "Answer me! Or make yourself useful and get upstairs and find the boy."

There was a dull thud in the darkness. Alfie turned around and tripped over something large and soft. As someone grabbed his neck and dragged him to his feet, he realized that Ashford was lying unconscious on the ground.

"No need for that, sister," snarled Murkle, dragging Alfie back through the cellars with ease as he kicked and struggled against her. "He wanted to save us the trouble."

There was a peal of laughter from Snitch. "Well, bring him quick," she called. "We've waited hundreds of years to bring about the new Age of Dragons. I won't wait a minute longer!"

Alfie went cold at Snitch's words. He had brought the key straight to them like a complete idiot. But how could they have waited that long? Were they not human?

"You set the school stage on fire, didn't you?" he panted, struggling against Murkle's grip on his neck. "You did it while you were away so that no one would ever think it was you. You could have killed people! Do you even care?"

"We knew we could rely on your generous nature. So good of you to offer an alternate venue when you thought we were out of the picture. How else would we get a chance to wake the rest of our brothers and sisters?"

"You think dragons are your brothers and sisters? You're mental! What about Jimmy? He nearly died!"

"You think we'd lose sleep over one less brat?" spat Murkle. "He's lucky we sounded the alarm. We wouldn't want to burn the whole school down—it has been our home for so many, many years. It's just a shame it's always infested with children."

As Murkle began to rant about the many things she detested about children, Alfie recognized the cool air and mossy smell of the chamber where Robin had fallen into the pool. Barely stopping to think, he swung his flashlight upward as hard as he could. There was a crunch as it connected with Murkle's chin, cutting her off mid-sentence. She stumbled and loosened her grip. Alfie kicked out sharply, knocking her into the dark water.

"Quick, sister," she screamed as she tried to splash her way out of the pool. "Head him off!" Her sentence ended in a gurgle as the current caught her, dragging her down below the surface.

Snitch's footsteps echoed behind Alfie as he ran through the darkness. He knew he was going in the right direction when he tripped over Ashford for the second time. He wanted to stop but had no choice but to run for the steps, hoping that Ashford would be okay until he could send help. Snitch burst out of the shadows and made a grab for him. He dodged. Her nails raked his calf as he started up the stairs. She hung on tightly to his ankle, but he yanked his leg loose, kicking out with both feet. Her eyes seemed to glow yellow in the darkness as she snarled up at him, revealing long, pointed teeth. He threw the dead flashlight as hard as he could in her direction and scrambled up the stairs.

The heavy door swung shut behind him as he reached the upper cellars, silencing a shriek from Snitch. It was almost as if the castle was trying to help him by slowing her down. "Thank you!" he shouted over the noise of Snitch throwing herself against the door. It finally burst open with a bang just as he safely reached the stairs up from the undercroft. He bolted up them and into the kitchen, only to find his path barred by Hugo Pugsley's barrel chest.

"You should be in the hall," smirked Edward over his friend's shoulder.

"Out of the way!" shouted Alfie, frantically struggling to get past as he heard Snitch crashing through the upper cellars.

"Mrs. Salvador sent us to find you," said Hugo, dodging around to block Alfie's path. "You're supposed to lead the cast onstage at the end of the play."

"Move!" yelled Alfie, bowling them out of the way.

"You'll be in even more trouble when we tell her you did that," Edward called after him as Snitch burst into the kitchen.

"Miss Snitch," said Edward gleefully as he realized she was chasing Alfie. "We tried to tell Alfie he was supposed to be in the Great Hall, but he just shoved me out of the way." Alfie glanced back. Edward's smile had disappeared as he saw the savage look on Snitch's face.

"Run, you idiots!" screamed Alfie as he raced from the kitchens. There was a crash behind him but he barely had time to feel sorry for the two boys—a dripping Murkle had burst through the castle door. She screeched in anger as she made a grab for him. He nimbly dodged her charge and raced into the Great Hall, straight past the confused cast waiting at the back. Some of them ran along behind him while the others looked around, unsure what to do.

"Stop, Alfie!" hissed Robin, grabbing at his tunic. "The play isn't over. We're not supposed to go up yet!" Alfie could hear whispers spreading through the confused audience as he pulled away from Robin and sprinted down the central aisle. Cormac sat up from his deathbed, looking confused as Alfie invaded the stage, turning to see Murkle and Snitch bowling children out of their path as they charged after him.

"Listen, everyone!" Alfie shouted over the sudden uproar. "Murkle and Snitch have got everyone believing their lies. There's something wrong with them—you can't trust them. They're the ones that burned down the school hall!"

"Shut up and get down from there, boy!" screamed Snitch.

"This child attacked us!" roared Murkle as she turned to face the stunned audience. Alfie looked to his family as they looked from him to the headmistresses.

"He also stole something from us," said Snitch, as she looked out over the audience. Her eyes had taken on the same yellow color they had in the cellar. Her voice became much lower and calmer. "A necklace . . . it was ours and he stole it."

A murmur went through the audience. "He stole from his teachers? Alfie's a thief?"

"Don't listen to them!" Alfie yelled as he saw the familiar glazed expression begin to spread across all of the eyes in the hall in response to Snitch's tone and snakelike stare. "Don't look at them. They're hypnotizing you!" A couple of people started to boo him.

"He should give it back," added Murkle, adopting the same eerie tone as her sister. "He stole it and he should give it back."

"They're lying!" Alfie yelled, looking around for someone, anyone, who wasn't falling under his teachers' spell.

"Thief!" someone called.

"Stealing is wrong. Give it back, son," said his dad in a monotone as he stood up and turned to Alfie with a blank expression.

"They're lying, Dad," said Alfie, before raising his voice and shouting to the whole room. "They're liars, I can prove it!"

Murkle and Snitch scrambled up onto the stage and stormed toward him.

"Give us the talisman key!" they demanded. Their eyes bored into him, seeming to gleam yellow. He realized that they were trying to control him, but the hypnosis trick they had pulled on everyone else wasn't working. Could the talisman be protecting him from it, or maybe it was the magic inside him? Alfie reached around to the back of his belt, pulling out the two water pistols he had filled with Orin's potion. The two women roared with laughter.

"A strange time to play games, little boy!" cackled Murkle. They lunged toward him. Alfie aimed at their faces and pulled the triggers, trying to spray as much of the potion as possible into their screaming mouths.

"See this behavior," Snitch called out to the audience, wiping her face as she grabbed one of Alfie's arms. "First he steals from us, then this horrendous show of disrespect!"

Alfie's blood ran cold as the audience got to their feet, booing and yelling at him. Even his family looked as though they were about to join in. Murkle and Snitch's hypnosis had held. Why hadn't the potion worked? He realized that even if they admitted everything right now, it would be no use in front of this audience. He couldn't see any way back from this moment. Soon they would drag him down to the cellars, and no one would do a thing to stop them, not even his dad or the twins.

A crumpled program hit Alfie in the face as Murkle and Snitch dragged him from the stage to a chorus of taunts and jeers. He wondered if he could get away from them and hide in Orin's study—but as he twisted and tried to wrench himself free, he realized there was no getting away this time.

"Move, boy, or I'll ask your father to help us," said Snitch.

"Maybe your grandmother would like to help too," giggled Murkle. "Shall we ask her . . . ?"

A loud yowl interrupted her taunt, silencing the baying crowd. Alfie looked down to see Galileo standing in the aisle. His tail was puffed up like a chimney brush as his fur rose into a spine along his arched back. He yowled and hissed at the two women.

"What is wrong with that creature?" said Snitch, grabbing a program and launching it at the cat. Galileo sprang out of the way and continued to hiss. Snitch suddenly doubled over as though she had been struck in the stomach.

"Your face, sister," shrieked Murkle. Snitch's features appeared to be melting in and out of focus. Murkle clutched at her own face, which was also distorting. Alfie saw his chance and pulled away from the sisters.

"He did something," she cried, launching herself toward Alfie. "What did you do to us?" Alfie leapt back as Murkle dropped to the floor. He watched in horror as their bodies began to contort along with their faces. The potion was only supposed to reveal the truth. Had he just poisoned his headmistresses in front of everyone?

Alfie stared. Murkle and Snitch had gone, and in their place stood two men. They were a similar size and shape to the two sisters and just as mean-looking.

"Mr. Smeadon? Mr. Lurcher?" said Granny, getting up and looking at the men in surprise.

"What have you done, boy? Stop this now!" the two

men demanded, their mouths moving together as they spoke in exactly the same voice. The rest of the crowd started to come out of their trance as the two figures began to contort and change again, briefly settling on a new form.

"That's Miss Craggs and Mr. Fargle," said Hexbridge's oldest resident, Ernie Wilmslow, rolling down the aisle in his wheelchair. "Ain't seen those two for over eighty years, but I'll never forget the hidings they gave me—couldn't sit down for a week!"

The changes became faster, different clothing and faces flickering across the two forms. Their faces became twisted and distorted—strange green-tinged parodies of human faces.

"What did you do, Alfie?" shouted Holly in horror.

"I . . . I don't know," shouted Alfie over the screaming of people scrambling to get out of the way of the horrifying transformation. "I only wanted to show you all what they're really like. I had to stop them!"

A terrible gurgling came from the two bodies as they blurred into one mass and began to grow. The gurgling turned into a deep rasping laugh as something huge materialized right in front of everyone's eyes.

Alfie staggered back in horror at the creature

looming over him. Murkle and Snitch weren't controlling the dragon, he realized at last—they *were* the dragon. And he had invited it in! People were screaming and scrambling over chairs to get away from the creature that had appeared in their midst. The two heads were pulling in different directions as the dragon seemed to be deciding who to eat first. Alfie knew he had to lure it away from the castle.

"Hey, sewer breath!" he called, hurling a chair at it. "You want this?" He shook the talisman at them. A rumbling growl came from the creature's throats. Alfie backed toward the doors, hurling another chair. The dragon bellowed, its clawed feet crunching golden chairs into firewood as it lumbered toward him. "Well, you'll have to come and get it!" Alfie yelled as he turned and ran from the hall.

CHAPTER TWENTY-ONE

An Unkindness of Ravens

Reaching the courtyard, Alfie pulled the silver whistle from his pocket and blew it as hard as he could. Within seconds, Artan had swooped down from the tower and scooped him up onto his back.

"Quick, get us away from here before it kills someone!" Alfie lay flat and grasped the bear's fur. Artan shot up into the sky just as the dragon burst through the castle doorway and launched itself after them.

"You want to be more careful picking your guests," roared Artan as they rocketed into the air, the lights of the castle dwindling below as they soared over Lake Archelon. The moon reflected off the water, illuminating the dragon as it flashed past. Artan swooped downward, almost skimming the lake as he dodged the tail that whipped toward them. Alfie hung on tight as the bear wheeled to the left. They gained a few precious seconds as the dragon flapped around, struggling to turn as quickly as the bear.

"Where to?" called Artan.

"The forest!" Alfie shouted. The dragon would be too big to follow—maybe Artan could lose it among the trees. They shot past the castle again and headed toward the village. Alfie saw his cousins racing down the hill with Jimmy and Holly, trying to follow their flight path. The adults were milling around on the drawbridge, still looking dazed. A clatter of breaking tiles came from behind them as the dragon landed briefly on the church spire, then launched itself in their direction.

"Look out!" he screamed as the dragon whistled through the air, wings flat to its sides as the spire crashed to the ground behind it. Artan dodged a second too slowly this time, and its great tail lashed against them. As they dropped from the sky, the bear wrapped himself around Alfie, softening his fall as they crashed into the village square.

Alfie leapt to his feet, grimacing as his ankle buckled under him. The dragon landed with a thump, claws clattering on the cobbles. It stomped a foot onto Artan's back—pinning the bear in place as he struggled to take flight.

The head with the sharpest snout dipped down to within two feet of Alfie. As its pupils narrowed to slivers of black in its yellow eyes, he knew that he was looking at Snitch.

"The talisman key," it snarled, extending one of its claws toward him.

"No," said Alfie. He backed away, trying not to show the pain he felt as he put weight on his ankle.

"Wrong answer!" boomed the dragon, sending a searing blast of air from its nostrils. Alfie staggered back from the hot, sulfurous stench. "Idiot child! Did you really think that you could stand in the way of us taking it back whenever we wanted?" The dragon picked Artan up between two claws and dangled him in the air. Lizardlike frills unfolded with a snap around the two heads, vibrating threateningly as the beast examined the bear. "So old and dried out," it observed.

"One little spark and . . . *poof!*" cackled the fat scaly head that had Murkle's sly features.

"Put him down!" screamed Alfie as smoke began to curl from Snitch's nostrils. Glaring up at the dragon, he became aware of a whispering noise building up inside his head. His skin tingled and a warm sensation flowed through his veins.

The dragon had stopped toying with the bear. Both of its heads were turned to Alfie, their eyes wide and glittering.

"Look at his eyes," the heads hissed to each other. "It's Orin's magic. It wasn't lost. *He* has it."

Orin's magic! It was awake inside him, just like the day of the fire. But this was different from the school hall—he felt in control. He could almost understand it as it whispered to him, asking to be released. To be fed.

"We could take it," hissed Murkle, eyes gleaming greedily. "Feed it on the humans, their electricity lines and power stations. Then we could use it to rebuild the land for our brothers and sisters! Tall mountains, steaming volcanoes, lovely lakes of lava! The humans would farm their livestock, just for us. And the ones who won't . . ." Her forked tongue shot out and licked her lips greedily as she looked down at Alfie. He glared back. The whispering in his head was like the soft roar of a mighty waterfall.

"Or we could create a new breed of dragons," growled Snitch, baring her long fangs and sending out a snort of steam. Murkle's head snapped around to face her as she continued. "All the others ever did was fight. Why not leave the gateway sealed? Let them sleep forever. We'll build our own army of dragons . . ."

". . . with us as their rulers!" shrieked Murkle. "The world will be ours!"

Alfie tried to stay calm, but his heart was beating faster and faster. An immense feeling of power had filled his body. He felt stronger than he had ever felt before.

"So how do we get it?"

"Like this!" Snitch's head shot toward Alfie. Her jaws snapped shut on nothing but air as he rolled aside. Electricity crackled through his veins. If the magic fed on energy, he wondered, could he use it to draw out the dragon's strength, like Orin had used it to absorb Agrodonn's magic? He dodged Snitch's jaws again, fury building as he concentrated on the magic inside him. He had no choice—he had to use it.

The dragon lurched forward again and Alfie let go, imagining the full force of the magic bursting out of him, tearing into the creature. Immediately he knew that something was wrong. A massive electrical charge shot through his chest, throwing him to the ground. The dragon was completely unharmed and let out a deep rasping laugh from both of its throats as Alfie groaned from the pain of hitting the cobbles so hard. Before he could clamber to his feet, a claw jabbed down onto his chest, pinning him back to the ground. He cried out in pain as the tip of a talon slowly pierced his skin.

"Alfie!" yelled Robin, racing across the cobbles, closely followed by Madeleine.

"Get your claws off him!" screamed Madeleine, picking up stones and hurling them at the dragon with all her might. Murkle and Snitch's lips drew back into terrifying grins, revealing razor-sharp teeth as they ignored the stones bouncing harmlessly off their armored body.

"Remove the key first," Snitch growled as Murkle's teeth snapped within inches of Alfie's face. A claw hooked under the talisman as Alfie wriggled helplessly on the cobbles. The cord snapped and it flew across the square. Alfie stared into Snitch's gaping maw as she prepared to swallow him whole. Suddenly, the air between them was filled with black feathered wings and snapping beaks.

Alfie staggered to his feet and stared up in awe as hundreds of ravens flocked down into the square, heading straight for the dragon like tiny warplanes. The dragon snapped both sets of jaws, sending feathers flying as the birds pecked at its eyes, ears, and wings. For every bird it caught, ten took its place. The moon and stars were blotted from view as the swirling cloud of ravens descended on the dragon like an oily black tornado. The beast screeched and took to the air, sending jets of flame into the swarm, which parted and regrouped like a shoal of fish as it continued its attack.

"Quick, Alfie!" said Robin, pulling him to his feet. "Let's go while it's busy."

"I can't!" Alfie looked up at the ball of feathers surrounding the dragon and knew that Caspian was in there somewhere, saving his life. "I've got to stop it. The talisman, quick, help me find it!"

They spread out to search the cobbles. The charred bodies of ravens began to rain down around them as the battle raged overhead.

"Here!" called Madeleine suddenly. "Is this it?"

"Yes!" Alfie grabbed the talisman and checked that the lens was still intact. *The lens!* Emily had said that it could focus energy. Could it focus the magic too? He leapt aside and a jet of flame scorched the cobbles as he fastened the talisman around his neck.

"What now?" asked Robin, helping a dazed Artan float away from the flaming ravens that were dropping from the sky.

Alfie knelt down on the ground and closed his eyes, shutting out the noise of the battle as he focused, calming his mind and beating heart as the voice in his head became clear. Suddenly he knew what to do. He had used the magic too violently before. This time he listened to it and guided it, directing the buildup of energy toward the talisman. A warmth spread across the center of his chest.

Opening his eyes, he stood up. His ankle gave him no pain now. He felt calm and alert rather than seething with raw power.

"What are you going to do?" asked Madeleine.

"Shh! Let him concentrate," whispered Robin.

The ground was covered in the corpses of ravens that had fought to protect him. The survivors withdrew and swooped away. Alfie prayed that Caspian wasn't among the dead.

The dragon spun furiously in the air, spitting flames after the retreating birds. One of Murkle's eyes was closed and the creature's wings were in tatters from the hundreds of beaks that had torn at them. It steadied itself in the air and caught sight of Alfie standing below. Both mouths screeched in unison, sending out a fiery blast that turned the weather vane on the village hall into a molten stream of metal.

"*Run*, Alfie!" screamed Madeleine as it dropped toward him.

Alfie didn't move. He stared up into the eyes of the creature as it hurtled down through the night sky. With his mind fully focused on the talisman, he calmly took a deep breath and released the magic that begged to be free. It was as though he had released a ravenous beast from its leash as it flowed through him, exhilarated at being used. A beam of blinding white light shone out from the talisman as the magic poured out through his chest, channeled by the lens. Alfie felt invincible, as though he could do anything or have anything he wanted. *And why shouldn't you?* whispered a little voice at the back of his mind. *I can make your greatest dreams a reality . . .*

The dragon swooped down, terrible jaws gaping. The beam tore into it. A roar of pain filled the night as the light ripped through the creature's chest. Alfie closed his eyes instinctively before it crashed into him, and he heard a dull thump as something landed on either side of where he stood.

Alfie struggled against the dizziness he felt as the magic rushed back inside him, flowing back through the talisman to whatever secret place inside him it called home. It felt content, almost purring like a cat that had just been fed. Something about the sensation repulsed him, and he had to fight hard against the sick feeling rising from his stomach.

Robin was shouting something. Madeleine whooped with delight.

"You did it!"

Alfie opened his eyes. Lying on the cobbles, dazed and bloodied, were Murkle and Snitch, back in their most recent human form.

CHAPTER TWENTY-TWO

Weaving the Strands

"There they are," shouted a pompous voice. "I demand you arrest them at once!"

Lord Snoddington was marching across the village square with Inspector Wainwright and his officers in tow. Alfie thought he was one of the targets of his rage until the policemen dragged Murkle and Snitch to their feet. A bruised Edward and Hugo looked on from behind Lord Snoddington as he shouted, "The last person to lay a hand on a Snoddington swung from the gallows!"

The rest of the villagers had wandered down the hill from the castle and were standing dumbstruck in the village square, staring at the fallen spire and dead ravens.

"Alfie!" called his dad as he rushed over, followed by the Merryweathers. "What happened? I remember hearing shouting in the Great Hall, and then we saw fireworks down here. Lord Snoddington's son said that he was attacked by your headmistresses. Did they hurt you too?"

"They'll have me to answer to if they did!" added Granny. "I just wish I could clear my head—I feel as though I've been asleep for a week. For some reason I keep thinking about my old headmasters—they were almost as bad as those two." She nodded toward the headmistresses as they struggled and swore at the policemen who held them.

Snitch managed to get one of her arms free and made a grab for Alfie. She pulled her hand back with a yelp. Aunt Grace had given it a bone-crunching thwack with Uncle Herb's pipe, creating a little shower of red-hot tobacco embers. Snitch looked at her bruised and burned knuckles in horror as the officers handcuffed her to Murkle and led them both across the square to the police station. Alfie gave a wry smile as he realized that they no longer had a scrap of power left.

"Could someone explain what went on here?" asked Uncle Herb as he refilled his pipe. "One minute we're watching a play, then there's all this noise, and now we're in the square surrounded by these poor dead birds."

Alfie didn't answer. He had just spotted a familiar cloaked figure striding stiffly toward them.

"Caspian!" he called, running toward him. "Are you okay?"

"Just a knock," replied the lawyer, wincing as Alfie grabbed his arm.

"We'd all be dead if it wasn't for you and the other ravens," said Alfie. "You saved us. I don't know how to thank you!"

"Why would you need to do that?" said Caspian, raising an eyebrow. "I was merely guarding an asset our firm has been tasked with protecting."

"Me?"

"Saving your life was simply a side effect of ensuring continued containment of the magic that you carry."

Alfie could hardly believe that even after all the bloodshed, Caspian still sounded so utterly practical and indifferent. "Did you see what happened? The magic made Murkle and Snitch human again."

"They were never human to begin with," said Caspian. "The dragon had found a change magic that allowed it to alter its appearance. It had maintained a human guise for such long periods of time that it reverted to that form when your magic absorbed its own."

"So they can never turn back?" asked Alfie.

Caspian shook his head. "A magical creature, trapped

in two separate bodies for a human lifetime. I almost pity them."

Lord Snoddington had taken it upon himself to start ordering people around and was clearing a path through the square by kicking the raven corpses into a pile. He stopped and backed away slowly as Caspian's furious black eyes burned into him.

"Were they . . . like you?" asked Alfie.

"Part human? No, these were not shape-shifters, but they were the best of the bravest of birds. When Ashford summoned me they answered my call, ready to die in battle or earn a tale to tell."

"Is Ashford hurt?" asked Alfie, humbled by the sacrifice of the ravens.

"His pride hurts more than his body. For one such as him to be subjugated is rare indeed. He'll feel the sting for some time." A slight smirk flashed across Caspian's face, as if he took some slight pleasure in this. It vanished as quickly as it appeared and he flicked back his cape. "Now, to knit together the frayed ends in these people's minds before they unravel completely."

Alfie helped him as he herded together the people milling around the square and led them back up the hill to the castle.

"What are you going to tell them?" he asked, running to keep up with the lawyer's long strides.

"I'm going to help them put together a version of events that they are happy to believe," said Caspian. "The minds of most adults are not as flexible and resilient as yours. Theirs have been manipulated and played with and are desperate to latch on to something solid to fill the gaps. I will simply facilitate their choice of memory and repair the damage done."

Everyone flocked back into the Great Hall. Alfie was amazed to see that the chairs were undamaged and everything was back exactly where it had been. It was as if nothing had happened. People breathed sighs of relief, settling happily back into their seats, as things seemed slightly more normal at last. Ashford was leaning against the stage nonchalantly. He winked as Alfie caught his eye.

"Mr. Bone?" said Robin, as they were ushered to their previous positions at the back of the hall. "Do we have to be here for this? We've already spent two weeks being unable to believe the truth. I don't want Alfie to be the only one who remembers what happened this time."

"Who will he talk to if we forget this?" said Madeleine. "I hate knowing that Murkle and Snitch stole our memories and turned us against him. I'm just starting to remember some of the things we forgot. Don't make us lose this too."

Caspian turned to Alfie. "They have seen some of the power of the magic that you guard." His voice had taken on a very serious tone. "The more people who know, the more dangerous life could be for you. Can you trust them with so powerful a secret?"

Alfie looked at his cousins as they stared defiantly at the lawyer. He smiled. "Completely."

Alfie could hear Caspian begin to address the audience in a soothing, authoritative voice as they left the hall. He led his cousins out onto the drawbridge, where they sat dangling their legs down over the moat. Madeleine and Robin both seemed to be avoiding looking at him. Their eyes were fixed downward, watching the water rushing below their feet.

"We're so sorry!" Madeleine burst out suddenly.

"We should have believed you—"

Alfie cut Robin off before he could finish. "You don't need to apologize."

"But you must have felt so alone," said Madeleine, blinking back what might have been a tear. "I feel like we abandoned you."

"They did something to your heads—there was nothing either of you could do about it. If they hadn't done that I know you'd have been there for me, all the way."

"Always," said Robin, his face deadly serious.

"At least they can't mess with us ever again," said Madeleine. After a moment of silence, she added quietly, "That thing you did to them—was that Orin's magic?"

Alfie nodded. "It was weird—like it was alive. While I was using it, I . . ." He paused and looked down at his shoes dangling over the rushing water below. Robin and Madeleine waited patiently for him to finish. "I felt so good—like I should be using it all the time, letting it out to feed and then using it to create anything I want." He looked up from his feet. Madeleine and Robin were watching him in silence.

"But I wouldn't," he added quickly. "It seemed so satisfied and pleased with itself after it fed on their power. I felt sick. I wanted it out of me. I never want to use it again."

"If that's how it made you feel," said Robin at last, "then I think Orin was right to give it to you."

"Exactly," added Madeleine. "If Murkle and Snitch had taken it from you, there's no way they would have held themselves back from feeding it and using it to create every terrible thing they wanted. It makes sense that it should be guarded by someone who doesn't want to use it." She gave Alfie a squeeze. "Come on, cheer up! It's not every day you get to play King Arthur *and* slay a real dragon!"

"You've got a point there." Alfie smiled as he climbed to his feet. "Now let's go." He set off down the hill toward the village, turning to call back. "I need your help with something very important."

CHAPTER TWENTY-THREE

Christmas at Hexbridge Castle

"Hey, Alfie! Christmas dinner is on the table."

"Okay, Dad. We'll be there in a minute," called Alfie, his voice slightly muffled by the crisp white snow that blanketed the courtyard. He was sitting in the farthest corner of the garden, chipping away at a stone slab under an ash tree. Setting down his dad's hammer and chisel, he brushed away the snow and stone chips and sat back on his heels to examine his work. "Well, what do you think?" he asked.

On the slab was carved a jagged outline of a bird with its wings spread in flight. Under the image he had painstakingly chiseled out the words:

HERE LIES AN UNKINDNESS OF RAVENS, THE BEST OF THE BRAVEST OF BIRDS

"It's beautiful, Alfie," said Madeleine, placing a sprig of mistletoe on top of the earth mound in front of the slab.

"It's a strange word for them, isn't it?" said Robin, placing a sprig of holly next to the mistletoe. "An unkindness. Yet Murkle and Snitch would probably have destroyed the village and everyone in it if the ravens hadn't fought for you."

Alfie bowed his head and stood silently for a minute in front of the grave with Robin and Madeleine. Respects paid, they traced their own footprints back through the snow, following the delicious smells drifting from the castle. Icicles dangled from the branches of the great oak tree, sparkling in the afternoon sun.

Alfie still limped slightly from his twisted ankle. The raven grave, the pain in his ankle, and the healing claw mark on his chest were the only remaining traces of the battle that had been fought in Hexbridge only days earlier. Even the church spire had been mysteriously restored overnight. Alfie was very glad that he wasn't the only one to remember their adventures this time—although thanks to Caspian, the adults seemed to have forgotten all of the magical elements of the night of the school play. Their only memories were of Murkle and Snitch being arrested for going spectacularly off their rockers and attacking pupils during the performance.

"Hey, where did you guys go?" called Amy from the

top of the stairs as Alfie stamped the snow from his boots at the door. She had arrived at the castle with her gran the night before. Hopping onto the wide banister, she slid down toward him, somewhat faster than she seemed to expect thanks to Ashford's polish.

"Just saying good-bye to some friends," said Alfie, dropping his coat to catch Amy as she flew off the end of banister.

"Boots off and take your seats," said Granny, bustling past with a tray laden with jugs of bread sauce, red-wine gravy, and her special Christmas cranberry, tangerine, and cinnamon sauce.

The Great Hall looked like every Christmas fantasy rolled into one. A gigantic fir tree stretched almost from floor to ceiling, dripping with beautiful carved ornaments, colored glass baubles, and twinkling lights. The huge oak table was laden with a feast fit for a king and his entire court. There was a roast leg of lamb studded with garlic and rosemary, bowls of buttered sprouts, honey-coated carrots, crispy golden potatoes, a gigantic turkey, and a huge roast ham glistening with a honey glaze. Alfie sat down near a platter of little sausages wrapped in bacon and claimed six of the crispiest ones as quickly as he could.

Artan lay silent and grinning in front of the log fire that crackled away merrily in the hearth. Alfie could tell that the bear was enjoying watching everyone pull Christmas crackers and read out the silly jokes inside. Amy stuck on the false moustache and eyebrows from her cracker and wiggled them up and down until they fell into her potatoes. Ashford seemed quite recovered from being knocked out by Murkle but was under strict instructions not to do any work that day. Granny pushed him back into his seat every time he moved to help out.

Amy's gran, Lizzie, had made the most delicious desserts: plum pudding with chocolate-orange sauce, a fruity Christmas cake topped with a little village made out of marzipan and icing, and a heap of small spherical cakes dipped in white chocolate and coconut so that they looked just like snowballs.

After dinner, Alfie's dad revealed something he had been working on for months: a small solar- and water-powered engine. He had rigged it up to a large toy train that ran on tracks around the huge Christmas tree. Everyone applauded as the train tooted and began to puff and chug its way around the tree, steam billowing from its little funnel.

"Wow, Mr. B, look at it go!" said Amy as the train whizzed faster and faster around the track.

"You do know how to stop it, don't you, Dad?" asked Alfie as pine needles began to rain down from the tree with the heat of the steam. Before his dad could answer, the train flew off the track. The twins leapt out of the way as it whistled past them, shooting across the floor to smash into the far wall. The train gave one last shuddering gasp and wheezed into silence, except for the *tink-tink-tink* of cooling metal.

"Not bad at all," said Alfie's dad happily. "Definitely a lot more stable than last month."

Alfie shook his head and watched Ashford as he began working with Robin on the wooden puzzle cube the twins had bought him for Christmas. He realized that he didn't even know if the butler had any family of his own. He was still a mystery, but had been a great help in defeating Murkle and Snitch. Alfie wondered if he would have need of his help again anytime soon.

The responsibility of bearing the magic and living in a castle that guarded the last dragon gateway, and probably countless other secrets, was starting to weigh heavily upon Alfie. The feeling the magic had stirred inside him as he used it against the dragon had been terrifying. In that moment he had understood its power and how easily it could corrupt anyone willing to keep using it. No wonder Orin had sought to hide it. He hoped that somehow he would be able to meet the druid again soon. He had so much to ask and was starting to wonder if he would ever feel truly safe again.

"Think fast, Al!" shouted Amy. A ball of wrapping paper bounced off his face and into his pudding. Within seconds, a paper fight was in full swing. Alfie pushed all worries from his mind for today and threw himself into the battle. He had so much to be grateful for: loyal friends—both mortal and magical—an amazing home, but best of all, he had a family again.

Acknowledgments

There are many people who helped Alfie Bloom all the way from idea to print, and I am forever grateful for their support, feedback, and cups of tea. I'd like to take this opportunity to say thanks to:

Mum and Dad; you showed me new worlds within the pages of books and encouraged me to create my own. Thirty-four years later, here it is!

Those who visited Hexbridge first: Chris, James, Rebecca, Anoushka, Somduth, Elisabeth, Madeleine. You did a wonderful job of tidying the place up for everyone else.

Rhianna, for providing me with the most important writerly tomes and for teaching me the secret author fistbump.

Carol Anne, Andy, and Lucy; without our day trip to Castell Coch, the idea for this book might never have taken hold.

Ben and Helen, for believing in Alfie all the way.

About the Author

Gabrielle Kent is a writer and game design lecturer in England. She is a regular judge for the BAFTA Games Awards. On three occasions, she has been listed as one of the top one hundred women in the gaming industry, and in 2015 was awarded a Woman of the Year Award by *MCV* magazine. *The Secrets of Hexbridge Castle* is her first novel.